Rosa and Milo went back to the engine, where Milo let Rosa roll the charged orb in. The effect was immediate. As soon as the orb caught fire and started to spark with book magic, the Quip shot forward, meaning Rosa and Milo had to grab on to the nearest fixed bits of the train to stay upright. Rosa looked a little embarrassed again at the strength of her own imagination.

"Wow," Milo said. "I bet that means we'll get to Pages & Co. really, really . . ." But he trailed off as the inky darkness of Story started brightening. "I think we're here already," he finished in amazement. "It must be some serious book magic you're borrowing."

Rosa only smiled.

As the expanse of Story melted away, they rolled into Pages & Co., the Quip once again managing to tuck itself unobtrusively round the bookshelves. However, unlike the last t̶ ̶ ̶ ̶ ̶ ̶ ̶ ̶ ̶ ̶ hen the shop was closed and empty ̶ ̶ ̶ ̶ ̶ ̶ ̶ ̶ ̶ ̶ ̶ ̶ ̶ ̶ ̶ immer sun spilling in through the ̶ ̶ ̶ ̶ ̶ ̶ ̶ ̶ ̶ ̶ ̶ ̶ Pages family had not yet closed the ̶ ̶ ̶ ̶ ̶ ̶ ̶ ̶ ̶

And the problem with pe̶ ̶ ̶ ̶ ̶ ̶ ̶quent bookshops is that they tend to have very well-developed imaginations.

Which means
that a
large train
arriving in
the middle
of the shop
did not go
entirely unnoticed.

The Pages & Co. series

PAGES AND CO.
THE
TREEHOUSE LIBRARY

ANNA JAMES

ILLUSTRATED BY
MARCO GUADALUPI

PHILOMEL

PHILOMEL
An imprint of Penguin Random House LLC, New York

First published in the United States of America by Philomel,
an imprint of Penguin Random House LLC, 2023
First published in Great Britain by HarperCollins Children's Books, 2022
First paperback edition published 2024

Text copyright © 2022 by Anna James
Illustrations copyright © 2022 by Marco Guadalupi

Philomel is a registered trademark of Penguin Random House LLC.
The Penguin colophon is a registered trademark of Penguin Books Limited.

Visit us online at PenguinRandomHouse.com.

The Library of Congress has cataloged the hardcover edition as follows:
Names: James, Anna (Anna Lois), author. | Guadalupi, Marco, illustrator.
Title: The treehouse library / Anna James ; illustrated by Marco Guadalupi.
Description: New York : Philomel Books, [2023] | Series: Pages & Co. ; 5 |
Audience: Ages 8–12. | Audience: Grades 4–6. |
Summary: With his uncle Horatio trapped in an enchanted sleep by the
power-hungry Alchemist, Milo sets off with Alessia to find a cure with the help
of the Botanist, and in their hunt for an antidote, they must forage in the Secret
Garden, challenge Robin Hood, and confront the mighty Jabberwock.
Identifiers: LCCN 2022053817 |
ISBN 9780593327234 (hardcover) | ISBN 9780593327241 (ebook)
Subjects: CYAC: Books and reading—Fiction. |
Characters in literature—Fiction. | Magic—Fiction. | Libraries—Fiction. |
Fantasy. | LCGFT: Fantasy fiction. | Novels.
Classification: LCC PZ7.1.J3847 Tr 2019 | DDC [Fic]—dc23
LC record available at https://lccn.loc.gov/2022053817

Printed in the United States of America

ISBN 9780593327258

1st Printing

LSCC

US edition edited by Cheryl Eissing. • US edition designed by Ellice M. Lee.
Text set in Adobe Caslon Pro.

For Claire, who believed in bookwandering
from the very beginning.

1

No Ordinary Train

The train rattled gently beneath Milo Bolt as he stared out at the great expanse of darkness surrounding him. Through the windows of the Sesquipedalian he could see only inky nothingness, interrupted occasionally by a burst of glittering shadows. For the Sesquipedalian, or the Quip for short, was no ordinary train. Powered by ideas, it could take you anywhere you could imagine. And Milo was its Driver.

This was a very new state of affairs. It was only hours before that his uncle Horatio, book smuggler of note, had been in charge of the Quip, but it felt like a lifetime ago. A poisoned book and an alchemist intent on controlling all the world's knowledge had turned Milo's world upside down. Now the Driver's whistle was Milo's, and he was the only person who could tell the train where they were headed next. And he'd chosen to set out on his own, slipping away from Tilly and Pages & Co. quietly, with only—

"Milo?" a voice called.

"I'm in here," he shouted back, and a few moments later a pale face popped round the door to the engine room. Alessia was the Alchemist's daughter, which was just about as complicated as it sounds. She'd stolen away from her father's home in Venice on the Quip—and also stolen a lot of his research and recipes while she was at it. This was just as well, for Horatio was currently lying poisoned and unconscious in the Pages family's spare bedroom, and the only way to revive him was with the recipe in Alessia's notebook.

"What are you doing in here?" she asked, looking around the cramped, stuffy engine room.

"Habit, I suppose," Milo said, stretching his arms. Until very recently, he had spent a lot of his time keeping the engine topped up with the wooden orbs charged with imagination that kept the Quip traveling smoothly through the world of Story. Now he had the run of the train without anyone to tell him off, and yet it still felt like he was trespassing when he used Horatio's office. Even though he could have slept in one of the fancy guest carriages, Milo was staying put in his cozy, cluttered quarters right toward the back of the train. Alessia, however, had immediately and happily installed herself into the finest guest car, decorated with richly embroidered hangings and jewel-colored cushions.

There was barely enough room in the engine cab for Alessia to sit down next to Milo on the floor.

"Do you reckon they've noticed we're gone yet?" she asked.

"I suppose so," Milo said, thinking about the noisy Pages family kitchen they'd just slipped away from. "It's been at least an hour, right? I bet we'll get a letter in the postbox before too long."

"Will they ask us to come back?" Alessia wondered.

"I'm not sure. I hope they understand why we've left . . .

Tilly will, at least. But I am feeling a little bad about abandoning my uncle with them without asking."

"They'll look after him well," Alessia reassured him, "better than we could by ourselves here. They'll understand."

Milo knew she was right, but he couldn't quash the lingering guilt about leaving his poisoned uncle with a family he really barely knew. Horatio had only ended up at Pages & Co. in the first place because Milo had insisted that the one stolen dose of the Alchemist's antidote be used for Tilly's grandad first. He had been the first victim of the poisoned book, but he was awake and recovering now. This at least demonstrated that they could probably trust the recipe Alessia had smuggled away from her father in Venice. Not that they had any of the ingredients they needed to actually make it.

Horatio wasn't even supposed to have been poisoned—he would still be awake if he hadn't been trying to stop Milo from touching the tainted book.

"I can see you doing it again," Alessia said, poking him gently in the arm.

"What?"

"Feeling guilty about literally everything, despite nothing being your fault."

"Well, I'm not sure *nothing* is—"

"Truly, Milo," Alessia interrupted. "Have you ever poisoned a book?"

"No."

"And have you used book magic in experiments to try and take over the world?"

"No."

"And have you lied about your family in order to . . . Well, Horatio's motives remain as mysterious as ever. But, for the purposes of this exercise, have you ever lied about your family to someone who would actually like to know the truth?"

"Nope," Milo said with a small, reluctant smile.

"Your honor, I rest my case," Alessia said. "Stop blaming yourself for things that you didn't do. It's neither of our faults that we have what I will politely call less-than-ideal father figures."

"Yours is your literal father," Milo pointed out.

"I try to pretend otherwise," Alessia sighed. "He's not exactly the sort of role model a girl wishes for. At least Horatio seems to have looked out for you in some ways; he definitely was trying to keep you away from *my* father at the bare minimum. Although it's quite fun to think that it's probably both of their worst-case scenarios that we're now friends and have run away with the Quip. I for one take plenty of comfort in that."

Milo was not a person naturally inclined to see humor in stressful moments and so found Alessia's ability to make a joke out of almost everything a little alarming at times, not to mention her seemingly unflappable confidence. The only time he'd seen it crack was when she'd confessed that while she had the recipe to make the cure for Horatio, she had no idea what most of the ingredients were, let alone where to find them or how to actually put them together properly. They knew that Alessia's father tailored his potions and poisons to individuals to make them more potent—as well as harder to cure.

All of that was why they were currently on their way to Northumberland to find the one person who might be able to help with the whole mess—the Botanist.

2

Stories Are Made to Be Retold

Milo and Alessia sat with a piece of paper between them on the table in his uncle's office—a note they had found from the Botanist that hadn't reached Horatio before he was poisoned. They both had their hands cupped round steaming mugs of hot chocolate, topped with an above-average number of marshmallows.

The paper was thick and creamy colored, handwritten with swooping letters in emerald-green ink. It said:

Horatio,

I hope you are well. Please provide me with an update on your progress in discovering the poison compendium I inquired about. You know that we cannot continue with our work to

stop the Alchemist without its contents. I know that your mother is also eager to see you; it has been too long since you visited.

Best,
R

They were almost completely sure that *R* stood for Rosa, the true name of the mysterious Botanist who was the Alchemist's sworn enemy and a client of Horatio's. The poison compendium was sitting next to the note on the table. It looked like a very large book at first glance, with an illustration of a skeleton on the cover and its pages held together by two heavy gilt clasps. But if you opened those clasps, the cover swung open to reveal not paper and words but many tiny drawers and bottles housing dried flowers, plants, and berries. Alessia was familiar with some of the names on their labels and had pointed out those she knew to be deadly, though many meant nothing to her and others were unlabeled entirely.

"So, Horatio was after this all along, for the Botanist?" Alessia said as she opened one of the drawers and peered inside as though its contents might have suddenly become clearly identifiable. "He definitely told you to take it to her? We're not falling into some trap by doing it?"

"It was the last thing he said before he passed out," Milo confirmed.

"And apologies for the recap, but just to be clear in my own mind, you and Tilly then decided to take it to my father, noted evil genius, instead?"

"Okay, okay, we didn't know that bit at the time," Milo said defensively. "We thought he was the only one who could help cure Tilly's grandad and Horatio. To be fair, we *were* right about that!"

"I suppose it did work out well for me that you came to Venice." Alessia shrugged, and Milo knew that she'd rather he not fuss about how much it meant to her that she'd been able to escape on the Quip. He was more than happy to let her continue to appear nonchalant and lighthearted about it. After all, as she said, he'd take a morally dubious book smuggler for an uncle over a megalomaniac mastermind for a father any day—not that he knew much about his actual father. But that was the other reason he was so keen on finding the Botanist. According to the note, Horatio's mother, and Milo's grandmother—someone he had thought long dead—was with her.

The final items on the table between them were two large white books and a scrapbook bound in brown leather. On the spines of the white books were Alessia's and Horatio's names, embossed in gold. On the front of the scrapbook was Milo's name, written by hand in black ink.

"Have you looked at Horatio's yet?" Alessia asked, looking meaningfully at Horatio's Record. "It might have something useful in it, like where he's been hiding your official Record so he could keep track of your bookwandering."

"But we already know it's hidden on the Quip somewhere," Milo said. "It's the only place outside the Archive with enough book magic to track bookwandering. Well . . . I suppose the only place full stop, now."

Milo watched Alessia's eyes go to her ankle, which was wrapped in gauze bandages and still too sensitive for her to put much weight on. It had been stuck under a beam during the destruction of the Archive and its library of Records, which traced the book magic left by every bookwanderer whenever they traveled inside Story. Only a handful of Records had made it out safely: the two in front of them and the ones belonging to Tilly's family.

"I mean, we both know it's in his room," Alessia said, poking Milo's pocket where he kept his uncle's ring of keys and making them jangle noisily. "It's the only place he kept locked all the time."

"I know," Milo agreed. "I'm just building up to it. It's not like my Record will tell me anything I don't already know; it's a record of *my* reading life after all. This scrapbook has already told me much more."

"We should keep it close by anyway," Alessia pointed out. "We've seen how important the Records are. 'The record of the reader': that's what lots of my father's recipes talk about, and we saw how Archie's Record was the final ingredient that activated the cure. We need to keep all of ours safe."

"I'm just . . ."

"You're worrying about the other bookwanderers' Records," Alessia filled in. "I know. But what did I tell you about worrying over things that aren't your fault?"

"But that is *literally* our fault," said Milo woefully. "If we hadn't helped Artemis escape the Archive, it wouldn't have fallen down and vanished, and the Records would still be safe. What happens if we've doomed all of bookwandering? If— because we've destroyed the one way to save them—your dad can somehow poison them all?"

"Okay, well, firstly, I'm just going to say that I very much doubt that his plan is to individually poison every bookwanderer," Alessia said matter-of-factly. "I'm pretty sure he doesn't spend much time thinking about regular bookwanderers at all if they don't get in his way. Also, didn't you tell me the Archive was falling down *before* we helped Artemis do anything?"

"Yes, but . . ."

"Exactly," Alessia said. "It was going to disappear, and soon by the sound of it, regardless of what we did. I personally think it was Tilly's fault, somehow. I like her a lot, but she does seem to leave a trail of chaos in her wake."

"That's rich coming from us," Milo pointed out.

"Well, regardless, if we hadn't been at the Archive then we

wouldn't have rescued *any* Records, much less Tilly's grandad's to wake him up. There's also the fact that if it wasn't for us, who knows if Artemis would have been able to escape or find any kind of peace. She would have quite probably been trapped without us. So, I think, all in all, I'm going to chalk it up as a resounding success."

"Let's not get carried away," Milo muttered.

"We're basically heroes," Alessia went on, warming to her theme. "Benefactors. Saviors. The Robin Hoods of the book-wandering world. Stealing from the rich and giving to the poor."

"In this scenario, who are the rich and the poor?"

"My father is obviously the rich, and we've stolen his knowledge and his secrets, and the poor is . . . us?"

"That doesn't sound very noble to me," Milo pointed out.

"These things are flexible." Alessia grinned. "Stories are made to be retold."

As per usual, Milo felt a flustered mix of frustration and admiration at Alessia and her general perspective on life.

"Now, time to finally look in your uncle's room, yes?"

"Fine," Milo said, pulling out the ring of keys, knowing the only reason he was stalling was his own fear of what they might find.

3

A Few Questions

Milo approached the gap between the two carriages. There were only a few inches of space separating the doorway he was standing in from the locked door that led to Horatio's private carriage. Milo had only been inside it once, straight after Horatio had touched the poisoned book and collapsed, and Tilly and he had awkwardly maneuvered his unconscious uncle onto his bed. Milo had barely glanced around the room at the time, but he was almost completely sure there wasn't anything dramatically out of the ordinary there.

Finding the correct key on the ring, Milo tried to calm his shaky hands as he slid it into the lock. It turned easily with a satisfying click, and the door swung open. The room was thankfully as unremarkable as Milo remembered. Tidy and sparsely decorated, it contained very little. Next to the bed was a wardrobe that held multiples of the outfit Horatio always wore: gray wool trousers, crisp shirts, boots, and black coats. The only other piece of furniture in the room was a slim desk tucked into one corner. A single fountain pen and its elegant pen holder were all that was visible on its surface.

"Have you checked the drawers?" Alessia said from behind Milo, making him jump.

"I didn't hear you follow me," Milo said, calming his breathing.

"I hope that's okay," Alessia said, enthusiastically rattling the top desk drawer. "I thought you might need some encouragement to rifle through your uncle's private possessions. Bad behavior seems to sit uncomfortably with you."

"That's why it's called bad behavior," Milo said.

"Yeah, but who decided what's bad and good anyway?" she retorted, and Milo gave up. He was quickly learning it was a fruitless activity to try and win an argument with Alessia. Especially one about morality.

"Pass me the keys?" she said, holding a hand back over her shoulder. Milo did so and watched as she quickly and efficiently sorted through them and picked out the right key for both drawers on her first try. She didn't seem to expect praise or comment on her ability to do this, and moved out of the way once they were open without looking inside.

The top drawer held a collection of matching leather-bound notebooks, tied together with cords. The bottom drawer only had one item inside: a white hardback with the name Milo Avi Bolt stamped on its side.

"This feels . . . anticlimactic?" he said, holding the book in his hands. "I was sort of expecting something . . . different, but of course my Record is just the same as all the others."

"It's quite thin, isn't it?" Alessia pointed out.

"Horatio didn't like me bookwandering much," Milo explained. "He always wanted to know where I was. Partly so your father wouldn't find out about me, I suppose. Then Horatio could keep pretending that I wasn't going to inherit the Quip."

"Do you want to check the rest of the room?" Alessia asked.

"Let's just get these back to the office," Milo said. "I want to have a look at the notebooks." He piled the matching notebooks on top of his Record, and the two of them took it all back to add to their collection of information in Horatio's office, in the hopes that answers about exactly what Horatio knew might start presenting themselves.

Before he turned his attention to the notebooks, Milo flicked his Record open to the most recent page, expecting to see an entry about his last bookwandering trip to *The Wizard of Oz*, or even perhaps his visit to the Archive. But, instead of the lines of neat writing he'd seen in other Records, the page looked as though it had been written on in ink and then dropped in the bath. Except not quite—the paper was dry to the touch, and entirely smooth and unwrinkled. It was only the words that had been affected. They were no longer legible, just a smudgy black mess.

"That's . . . unexpected," Alessia said, peering over at the page. "Is there another reason Horatio was keeping this hidden, do you think? Are you . . . broken in some way maybe?"

"What?" Milo said, feeling cold all over. "You think I'm *broken*?" This was like being back under Horatio's observation, his words always sharp and full of hidden meanings.

"Not you personally, silly," Alessia said. "Just your bookwandering."

"Isn't that sort of the same thing?" Milo said, and he was worried he was going to start crying. Alessia seemed to sense that she'd got it wrong.

"Oh, I'm sorry," she said, her face twisting in worry. "I just meant, perhaps there's something Horatio knows about you or your bookwandering that he didn't want anyone else to know. You know, like how Tilly is."

"Tilly is special, not broken," Milo said.

"I bet she didn't always feel like that," Alessia mused. "But, anyway, 'broken' was the wrong word, I'm sorry. Special." She paused. "That's what I was trying to say," she added earnestly. "Maybe you're special like Tilly."

"I'm definitely not special—I just bookwander normally," Milo said, still a little shaken, if slightly reassured. The only thing he felt sure of was that he wasn't special in any way. He knew Alessia didn't mean to hurt his feelings. They were still learning how to be good friends to each other, and Milo's desire for acceptance was smashing right into Alessia's determination that *she* didn't need it.

Milo turned back through the pages of his Record, feeling more and more unsettled as he saw that almost all the pages were the same inky mess.

"Should I bookwander somewhere, and you can check if anything comes up like it's supposed to?" Milo asked desperately.

"Uh, hang on, I think we have a bigger problem than that," Alessia said as she held open her own Record, which looked exactly the same as his. A messy scrawl of blurred, illegible writing covered the pages.

Milo was ashamed to admit that his immediate response was one of relief. He wasn't broken, or if he was, then Alessia was broken in the same way. But his relief turned to fear as he grabbed for Horatio's Record. He yanked it open at random and felt sick at the same sight.

"Will it still work for the cure if it's like this?" he asked Alessia, whose face was pale, having clearly asked herself the same question. Her father's cure for the poison required the record of a reader; the cure would do nothing until it had this final crucial element, which tied it to the person it had been made for. They had burned a page of Tilly's grandad's Record and added the ashes to the one dose they had stolen from the Alchemist. While Milo had undeniably rather complicated feelings about his uncle, there was no world in which he didn't want to wake him up. And not just to answer a few questions about what on earth was going on.

"I don't know about the cure," Alessia admitted. "It's a combination of science and book magic, and I only understand a little bit of both."

Milo still felt queasy. They had gone to so much effort to get these Records, destroying the Archive at the same—

He paused.

"It's the Archive, isn't it?" he said, putting the pieces together. "When we helped Artemis leave, we took away the last bits of book magic holding the place together. It was only the sheer quantity there that made the Records work. That's how they could follow the book magic we leave in the stories we wander into. I don't know why we didn't think of it—how were the Records ever going to work without the Archive?"

"But there's no way we could have expected them to just disappear like this!" Alessia said. "Even if the Records stopped tracing our bookwandering going forward, we couldn't have predicted they'd start . . . dissolving. Anyway, I thought you said yours still worked on the Quip because there's so much book magic onboard!"

"That's what Artemis told me," Milo said, trying to remember the details. "But I don't think there's nearly as much here as there would have been at the Archive; the whole place was built of book magic, carved out of layers of Story itself. This is a real train made of metal and wood and whatever else trains are made of—even if it is powered by imagination. There must have been enough book magic here to make the Records work when they were still tethered to the Archive. But that place is gone now. It's like we've taken the batteries out of the book magic. What are we going to do?"

Milo felt himself starting to panic and tried to keep control of his breathing.

"I guess we have to hope the Botanist really knows what she's doing," Alessia said, looking out of the window at the inky darkness of Story.

"Are

we

nearly

there

yet?"

4

Everyday Magic

The rest of the journey passed quickly and anxiously. Milo started to read Horatio's notebooks, but they didn't mean anything to him. They seemed to be written in code or shorthand of some description. Although he could understand some individual words, he couldn't follow any thread to work out what was being recorded. The letter "M" cropped up regularly, and Milo tried to tell himself it could stand for many things apart from his own name, but he could pick no coherence or logic out of the writing as a whole.

Thankfully, before long, Milo could feel the telltale signs that the Quip was getting close to their destination. He had only been the Driver for just over a day, but already he was much more in tune with the Quip and how it was feeling. He could sense a ripple of enthusiasm spread through the train as they approached the final straight, just as he had noticed its anticipation when he set their course at the beginning of the journey.

Right now, the Quip was telling him they were very nearly there, and the darkness started to melt into light. The train chugged gently outside the limits of Story, as though it was nothing so spectacular to traverse beyond its edges, and suddenly they were in the wilds of Northumberland. As far as Milo and Alessia could see were crisp blue skies and rolling hills broken up by stone walls and herds of meandering sheep. From the windows on the left, they could make out one narrow road that wove across the countryside, with dark specks of houses or small villages just visible. To their right were only hills undulating across the skyline, edged by the silhouette of a crumbling wall.

"Hadrian's Wall," Milo pointed out to Alessia as the two of them stared through the window at the ancient Roman wall. They could see a path winding alongside its remains and every so often a pair of hikers climbing up and down the hills, following the line of the stones.

"They can't see us?" Alessia asked.

"Nope," Milo said, proud of his ingenious train. "People don't tend to see what they're not expecting; they'll either see a regular train chugging its way to the Lake District, or they won't notice us at all."

The Quip started to slow as they passed a small farmhouse and a coppice of tall, elegant trees.

"Here we are," Milo said quietly as a familiar sight came into view. He'd been to this spot several times with Horatio. He'd never been allowed off the Quip before, but he knew exactly what he was looking for—it was hard to miss.

"Come on," he said, his worry at what they were going to do without the Records temporarily muted by his excitement at showing Alessia. She followed him off the train, onto the soft grass where they had stopped.

In the middle of an almost perfectly symmetrical dip between two hills stood a majestic sycamore tree. There were no other trees nearby, and the tumbling wall spilled down one side of the hill and leaped up the other, forming a gentle curve at its base nestling the tree.

Milo locked the door to the Quip, and the two of them walked toward the tree without speaking. There was an overwhelming sense of tranquility around it, and as they got closer they could hear rustling as the gentle breeze moved its leaves.

"Oh, you can feel the magic here, can't you?" Alessia said, reaching out and placing a hand softly against its bark.

"I don't think the tree itself has anything to do with book magic," Milo said.

"I don't mean book magic," Alessia said, gazing up into the whispering leaves. "I mean regular magic, real-life magic—the kind that's all around. That everyone can feel."

It was true that there was something in the air here, somewhere it was easy to understand that the border between real life and imagination was not so solid at all. In front of the tree was a circle of stones set into the ground, like some kind of ancient firepit or marking.

"I wonder what that is," Milo said. "Is it to do with the Botanist?"

"Well, we can ask her if we find her," Alessia said. "Where do we go from here?"

"I don't know," Milo reminded her. "I've never been off the Quip before; I've never even been this close to the tree. We should head back to that farmhouse—maybe she lives there. I don't think we passed anywhere else she could live nearby, and Horatio definitely stopped at this tree."

"Let's head that way," Alessia agreed. "Worst-case scenario is that it's empty, or a normal farmer lives there. We can always ask them if they have neighbors."

The path followed the wall closely, snaking up the hill opposite the Quip. Once they had crossed the wall, they could see that the hill fell away fairly steeply on the other side, down to a shining lake, trees covering the slope down to the water. The climb up the hill was steep, and in the midday sun the two of them were soon sweaty and tired. Milo could see Alessia's limp getting more pronounced as they went, but she just shook her head at any inquiries into how her ankle was, so he simply made sure to stay behind in case she tripped and fell. Despite his worries, the fresh air and the sight of Northumberland sweeping out around them filled Milo with wonder.

"You can see why the Romans built this here, can't you?" Milo said breathlessly as they climbed a section of steps cut into the stony path. "It would be pretty hard to sneak up on them. I wouldn't like to meet a load of Roman soldiers at the top."

"Was it to keep people out?" Alessia asked.

"Yes, the Scots, I think, although I don't know that they were called that way back when," Milo said, trying to remember the few details Horatio had told him. It had always been a stop that had captured his imagination, and he'd yearned to be able to get out of the Quip and explore. "I'm sure the Botanist knows all about it."

By this point they'd reached the top of the hill and were relieved to see that the path flattened out as it, and the wall, disappeared into the pine trees they'd spotted from the Quip. If anything, the magical feeling was only increasing, but Milo couldn't tell if it was what Alessia called regular, everyday magic, or whether he could sense some sort of gathering book magic.

Both, perhaps.

The trees stretched up into the sky, sunlight filtering down as Milo and Alessia crunched along the gravelly path. Through the trunks they caught the odd glimpse of the lake at the bottom of the slope. It was so peaceful, and Milo wished they were here on less urgent business.

They had reached a particularly dense portion of the woods, Alessia leading the way, when Milo heard a rustle in the grass. Reaching out, he gently grasped Alessia's shoulder. She turned slowly, her head tilted, questioning why he had stopped her. Milo cupped his hand behind his ear and then pointed at the place he thought the noise was coming from.

"I heard something," he whispered. "A rustle. There! I feel like we're going on a bear hunt!"

"Is it just the wind in the grass?" she said very quietly.

But then there was the unmistakable sound of tiny paws scampering on bark, and a red squirrel darted out of the foliage and along a branch that ran just above their heads. At the same moment, the grass where the rustling was coming from parted, and out stalked a slender fox, its russet fur matching the squirrel's almost exactly. It stood underneath the branch the squirrel was on, and the two animals simply looked at the two children.

"Uh, is that normal?" Alessia asked, staring at them in wonder. "Are they not used to humans?"

"I don't know what's normal for squirrels or foxes," Milo whispered. "I grew up on a train."

"Well, I grew up in a floating city," Alessia pointed out.

The fox and the squirrel were still looking at them intently. All of a sudden, the squirrel leaped down from its perch, landing gracefully on the stony path next to the fox, who didn't react at all.

"Okay, *that* can't be normal," Alessia said. "Don't foxes eat squirrels? It feels like they should."

"Do you think . . . do you think they can understand us?" Milo said. He faced the animals. "Hello?"

"Are you expecting the fox to talk back to you?" Alessia said, amusement in her voice.

"I don't know!" Milo said, feeling a little embarrassed. "I

thought it was worth a try at least! They might be talking animals from inside a book if we're near the Botanist!"

"But we're definitely *not* in a library or a bookshop," Alessia said. "As far as we know, only my father has worked out how to bookwander from anywhere else."

"I'm afraid one of those statements is not quite correct," a voice said from behind them, making Milo and Alessia jump. They spun round to see a redheaded woman standing on the path. She smiled warmly. "Welcome to the Treehouse Library. My name is Rosa, but I think you might know me as the Botanist."

5

The Treehouse Library

"Just to clarify," Alessia said, "which bit of what I just said is not correct? I really would like to know if these are talking animals."

"I'm afraid they're not," Rosa said. She was smiling, but Milo was very aware of feeling sized up. He wasn't sure how much she knew about either of them. "They're familiar sights around here," Rosa went on. "Not to mention well fed when they visit me in the library, but they are very much of this world."

"Do they have names?" Milo asked.

"No," Rosa replied gently. "We're very fond of them, but they're wild animals, not our pets."

Even so, Milo privately decided that they should be called Nutmeg (the squirrel) and Marmalade (the fox), and he would think of them as that until he was very old.

"The part that was wrong was saying that we're not in a bookshop or library," Rosa continued. "Although I am stretching the truth a little there, for dramatic effect. You gave me too good an opening. That said, we are very close to the Treehouse Library, where I live and work, and we can bookwander all we like from there. And very shortly we can make our way down, but before we go, do you mind if I just ask you a few questions? I want to make sure we're all . . . well, on the same page, if you will."

"Of course," Milo said, having expected as much, but he could feel Alessia bristle defensively next to him.

"Firstly—you are on your own?" Rosa asked. "Your uncle is not with you?"

"So . . . you know who I am?" Milo responded.

"Well, I probably should've made absolutely certain before saying anything at all," said Rosa with a smile. "But it wasn't hard to make an educated guess, and I could sense the Quip coming."

"What do you mean?" Alessia said, arms crossed.

"I can tell you more later," replied Rosa. "But I hope it's enough for now to say that I am very attuned to book magic, and as the Quip uses so much of it, it's impossible for me to ignore when she heads this way. But of course that also meant that I was expecting Horatio—and I had very much hoped to speak with him. Now, may I ask your name, Miss . . . ?" Alessia turned to Milo uncertainly, obviously worrying about the response to her surname. Milo shrugged, not wanting to conceal anything from Rosa that wasn't absolutely necessary to be kept secret.

"Miss della Porta," Alessia answered slowly, holding Rosa's gaze as if challenging her to react.

"I see," came Rosa's response. "I did wonder—Horatio had mentioned that he thought perhaps the Alchemist had a child. And I must insist on knowing a little more about your uncle's whereabouts, Milo."

"He is in London—at Pages & Co., a bookshop owned by our friends," Milo said. Rosa looked worried for a second before going back to her calm and interested expression. "He was poisoned by the Alchemist with a book meant for someone else," Milo explained. "But we have a cure, or at least a recipe, and . . ."

"And I had absolutely nothing to do with the poisoning, just to be extremely clear," Alessia interrupted. "I am on your . . . Well, I'm on Milo's side, that's for sure. So if you are too, I'm on your side. Deal?" Rosa failed to stifle a laugh.

"That's an alliance I'll gladly sign up for." Rosa smiled. "We must speak more of course, but your word is enough for me. Now, Milo." She paused. "Speaking of family, I'm not sure what you've been told or have discovered about . . ." She tailed off, not wanting to say the wrong thing.

"I know that . . . or I think that my grandmother is here?" Milo said quietly, not able to quite look at Rosa directly; the hope was too much to bear. His whole life, the only family member he had known or had any memory of was Horatio. The thought that there might be a whole extra person just through there, in the trees, had his whole heart in a grip.

"She is." Rosa smiled. "She'll be very happy to see you, I'm sure. Perhaps it's best if you don't mention for now that you arrived on the Quip, however."

"But why—" Alessia started to ask.

"We'll have plenty of time for questions, I promise," Rosa said. "Let's get somewhere more private, and much more comfortable. And perhaps on the way you can tell me the details about what has happened to Horatio and this cure."

Rosa turned off the path, down the hill into the trees. Milo and Alessia followed her as best they could, talking over each other as they explained the poisoned book and the recipe and their journey from Pages & Co. via the Archive. The slope was steep and covered in crawling tree roots and patches of dry soil where your feet could get carried away with themselves. Rosa noticed Alessia's limp straightaway and insisted she would take a look at her ankle as soon as they got somewhere safe, despite Alessia's protestations that she was managing fine. Milo could see her wincing in pain as they negotiated a particularly tricky stretch. Marmalade vanished into the trees ahead, but Nutmeg scurried along the branches above them, like a tiny red guard.

Milo couldn't quite place Rosa's age. Sometimes when he glanced at her face she looked to be not much older than them, her skin unlined and glowing, but then she'd turn and resemble an ancient woodland druidess, wrinkles deepening. He shook his head; it must be a trick of the light, or his weariness and worry affecting his eyes and brain. Her hair was a vibrant copper, and she had it woven into a thick braid that hung over one of her shoulders, tied at the bottom with a linen cord. Her skin was pale but sprinkled with freckles, and she was wearing loose-fitting dark-green overalls with a stripy T-shirt underneath, and white canvas sneakers.

After only a few minutes' walk down the slope, they reached a spot where the trees were crowded even closer to each other. They were nearly down to the lake, or Crag Lough as Rosa called it, and there was a line of Scots pine trees that were growing so closely together that they seemed like a wall.

"This way," Rosa said, grinning back at them. She approached a gap between two trees and reached a hand through some hanging vines, sweeping them to one side and ushering Milo and Alessia in front of her. For a moment Milo couldn't see anything except the curtain of leaves around his face and the trunks of two pines tight on either side, but then he broke back into the sunlight, and in front of him stood one of the most amazing things he'd ever seen. They were in a glade dappled with sunlight. The wall of trees enclosed the clearing on three sides, with glints of the lake visible a little way down the hill on the fourth. In the center of the glade was a cluster of trees, and among their branches was a treehouse.

"This is the Treehouse Library." Rosa smiled. "Come on up."

6

Gaps Where Stories Might Be Hiding

One particularly large tree stood out. Milo didn't know much about trees, but he could clearly see that it was different from the others, which were tall but thin with Christmas-tree-like needles. The central tree in the glade had a much thicker trunk and broad leaves instead of needles. He thought it might be an oak, as he was almost sure he could see acorns nestled among the leaves. Around its trunk spiraled stairs that reached up into its uppermost canopy. There were four levels that Milo could see, each with a platform circling the trunk and various wooden structures built among the boughs of the oak and out onto those of the pines so that the whole thing stretched across the trees. Wooden walkways connecting huts and cabins perched in the branches, but all of it looked distinctly too noticeable.

"How do you keep this private?" Milo said, staring up at

the treehouse in wonder. "I know it's remote here, but people must walk along the path quite a lot, right?"

"It's a clever mix of trees and perspective." Rosa smiled. Alessia raised an eyebrow to show that she didn't believe her. "Okay, yes, and a little bit of book magic," Rosa said. "There's an . . . above-average amount here, and we can use it to do some gentle trickery. The way the trees grow around the glade does help too. If people spot the treehouse they tend to think that they've imagined it—but in a lovely way. They'll think they went for a walk through a beautiful wood and their imagination supplied some extra details. Perhaps that they caught a glimpse of a child's abandoned treehouse and they are remembering it as they wish it could be. Anyone with a good imagination does that all the time anyway; we see gaps where stories might be hiding. And people with weak imaginations, which they haven't been exercising enough, well, they simply won't see it at all, just as they don't see your lovely train, Milo. Now, up we go. Actually, Alessia, do you want to wait here to rest your ankle? I'll drop Milo off with Lina and then be right back down with some homemade ointment that might help a little. I'll give you both a proper tour very shortly, but Milo, I imagine you're keen to see your grandmother straightaway."

Milo nodded and followed her up the stairs.

Rosa took him to the third platform, where bridges made of ropes and planks stretched out to small cabins perched in four of the pine trees.

"These are our sleeping quarters," Rosa said. "The one to the left will be yours while you're here. And that is mine." She gestured to her right. "The cabin behind us is currently empty, and *this* one is where your grandmother has been staying since she first came to me."

"I'm not sure we'll be here long enough to need bedrooms," Milo said. "We've just come to ask you about the cure and give you the poison cabinet."

"You have the cabinet?" Rosa asked in surprise.

"Yes! We brought it to you like Horatio told us to."

"Right," Rosa said, standing still. "I am very keen to see that, Milo, and to hear about this cure, but I think that it is best—yes, it is—that you meet your grandmother first. After that, I can see what I can do to help your uncle. It is possible, even, that the cabinet will also help on more than one front, perhaps even with the cure itself. I had been hoping that Horatio would be bringing me information about . . . Well, we can come back to that; let us find Lina and look at the cabinet and recipe and go from there. That's more than enough to begin with. Now, follow me."

They walked across one of the gently swaying bridges to a little cabin built among the branches—Milo could even see branches sticking out through the roof. It reminded Milo of a hobbit's house. Rosa knocked on the round green door.

"Lina? Milo is here." She turned to Milo and spoke quietly. "I'll give you and your grandmother a bit of time by yourselves while I take a look at Alessia's ankle, but do come down to the library when you're ready."

Milo could do nothing except nod. There was a big part of him that very much wanted Rosa and Alessia there; he felt completely overwhelmed—full of hope and confusion and a touch of fear. After all, the Alchemist had said that it was Milo's grandmother's fault that his parents had been killed in a hot-air balloon crash.

"Come in," a thin voice called from inside, and he took hold of the handle and opened the door.

The trunk of the tree climbed through the center of the circular room. When he first entered, it was hard to see much, as the curtains were drawn and the room felt dark and close in comparison to the sunlight and fresh breeze outside. As his eyes got used to the gloom, Milo could see that all the furniture was made to fit the curved edges of the room, including a large bed that took up much of the space. The curved side fitted to the wall of the cabin, and the straight edge faced out to the room, and propped up in it was an elderly woman with brown skin and white hair. She looked very small against all the pillows and blankets, and Milo noticed that her breathing was shallow, as if it hurt.

"Milo?" she whispered, looking at him as if he were a ghost.

"Yes," he replied. "It's me." He found he didn't know what to call her. "You're . . . you're my grandmother?"

"I am," she said, not taking her eyes away from him. "Oh, you look so very much like your father."

Milo took a tentative step forward, finding that now he was actually here, with Lina in front of him, the thing he felt mostly was awkward discomfort. He had no idea what to say to her. Small talk felt silly, but how did you launch into asking if your grandmother was really responsible for the untimely death of your parents?

"Did you . . . How long have you . . ." Milo struggled to put into words the question that felt most pressing. "Why didn't you ever get in touch? Why didn't you tell me you were alive, that you were here?"

"Oh, Milo," she said. "I didn't even know that you were alive until very, very recently. I don't truly understand why I was not told, but people have their reasons and their motives for all sorts of insensitive actions, don't they? Rosa assured me she only had suspicions for a few months. It would seem Horatio has done quite a good job of keeping you hidden away for a long time. I wonder what else he has kept hidden from us all."

"He . . . I think he didn't want the . . . Do you know about the Alchemist?" Milo asked, entirely unsure about what Lina knew or didn't know.

"Yes," she replied. "I know, well, not *all* of Rosa's secrets." She glanced up at the door as if Rosa might be listening there. "But I know much of what she works on, and her efforts to limit the powers of the Alchemist take up a great deal of her time and energy. And I lived a full life before I came here, so, yes, I know about him and his ambitions."

"I think—I think Horatio was trying to keep me safe from him," Milo said. "He made some sort of bargain. Did you know? Because the Alchemist wants the Quip, and Horatio knew he would kill me and . . ." Milo paused, remembering that Rosa had asked him not to mention the Quip.

Lina visibly perked up as soon as the words left his lips.

"Where is the Quip?" she said, sitting up straighter. "Is she here now? Did you drive her here? Does the whistle work for you?"

Milo didn't know how to respond and remained silent, wishing that Rosa had stayed.

"You look like a rabbit in a trap," Lina said with a noise that sounded unsettlingly like a dismissive snort, but she shrugged and let the subject drop, even though a "for now" hung in the air.

"Right, so, Horatio knew the Alchemist was prepared to kill me to get the—the Quip," said Milo, trying to carry on calmly. "But there's a lot going on that we couldn't work out, and then Horatio . . ." He paused again, not sure what to say about the poison and the unnatural sleep Horatio had fallen into. "Do you know about Horatio? That he's—"

"What? A sneaky so-and-so who would trick his own mother out of her livelihood?"

"Uh, no," Milo said awkwardly. "That he's been poisoned. By the Alchemist."

"Oh," Lina said, lying back on her pillows with a sharp exhale. "No, I didn't know that. That's interesting."

Milo couldn't help but think that "interesting" was a strange choice of word on hearing your son had been poisoned.

"So you came here by yourself?" Lina went on.

"Not quite," Milo explained. "I came with my friend . . . Alessia."

"And who is she?"

"Alessia della Porta," replied Milo.

"Della Porta, you say?" Lina looked intrigued.

"Yes, the Alchemist is—he's her father," Milo said. "But

we can trust her. She doesn't agree with him at all, or help him."

"Of course not," Lina said quickly. "Although he is an . . . interesting man, isn't he?"

"You keep saying things are interesting," Milo risked. "I'm not quite sure what you mean."

"Well, the world is an interesting place full of interesting people." Lina smiled. "People are not so easily sorted into simple categories of good and bad, in my experience. And Alessia's father is a very clever and ambitious man, even if he has some less appealing qualities."

"Like wanting to kill me?" Milo said with a waver in his voice.

"Quite," Lina said, as if he had simply commented on the weather. "Clearly he has some unsavory traits."

"He told me," Milo said awkwardly, feeling completely unbalanced by Lina, "that it was your fault my parents died, that you sent them off in that hot-air balloon." Milo was alarmed to find great waves of anger bubbling up inside him. He'd lived his whole life without knowing what had really happened to his parents, or why he'd been hidden away for so long on the Quip with only Horatio for company. The only person who'd told him anything was the Alchemist, and he was the worst person Milo had ever met, and now his grandmother was acting so differently from what he had hoped or expected.

Lina looked at him for a long time, and Milo felt that he was being assessed for a purpose he could not grasp.

"Please. Just tell me what happened," Milo said.

"I will," Lina said eventually. "I am not unwilling, but it is hard to know where to start, and this is not a simple story. Then again, perhaps it must begin where it may yet end—with the Quip."

She gestured for Milo to sit on the armchair by the bed, rearranging the blanket over her knees, and began her story.

7

A More Unorthodox Approach

"I inherited the Quip from my father," Lina said. "He was the one who made the train what she is today, who worked out how to use book magic to power her, let her slip between layers of imagination and travel through the world of Story. Most bookwanderers only have the most surface-level understanding of Story, or the true power of imagination. Even our Underlibraries focus on administration more than anything else: keeping track of bookwanderers, solving problems that arise, protecting Source Editions. Although I've heard a rumor that you've crossed paths with the Pages family—who have always taken a more unorthodox approach.

"My father was never content to simply use imagination to travel in and out of books. He knew there was more to it, that there was some great well of magic that was fueling book-wandering, that books were the way we shaped and siphoned the magic, not the originator. We talk a lot about imagination, but people don't understand quite how powerful it can be. It brings things to life, it destroys things, and it is as old as the very first people to walk this earth. Unfortunately, there are others who have realized that harnessing imagination can create vast power, others such as Geronimo della Porta. Your friend's father. I knew of him long before I came here. In fact, my life changed because I met him. I may have had some . . . lapses in judgment, but he was behind it all. It's his fault your parents are dead, Milo, not mine.

"I was only in my late twenties when I inherited the Quip, after my parents grew old and wanted to settle somewhere comfortable and safe—not a fate that has ever particularly appealed to me. I had long thought they were naive to use the Quip only to explore the realms of Story, that there were much cleverer uses for such a clever train. And so, I renamed it 'Evalina's Literary Curiosities,' and traveled the world offering ordinary people the chance to experience the power of imagination. Those who couldn't bookwander, who didn't even know such a world existed, could have a glimpse of this extraordinary gift we lucky few have. I could share the magic of bookwandering with everyone, and, to sweeten the bargain, support myself very comfortably.

"To begin with I played it safe. I set up the Quip like a

traveling circus, and people could pay to have dinner with their favorite characters, that sort of thing. Customers just thought we were offering an incredible theatrical event. Why would you ever believe you were meeting the real Jay Gatsby or Mr. Darcy? Of course, there were bookwanderers who knew about the Quip, and they could pay to go deeper inside Story. Although I never stumbled across the Archive during all those years of traveling. I had heard of it, of course, and I was always on the hunt for a map, but never found one. Even I began to think it might just be a myth.

"Then non-bookwanderers started to clamor for more; they ceased to be impressed by what they thought were simply good actors. So, I did the natural thing—bookwanderers *must* have contemplated it before but not had the courage to try. I started to experiment with taking non-bookwanderers inside of books. Of course, they're not in control; they can't read themselves in like we can; they can't pull characters out. Even regular book-wanderers can rarely do this once their bookwandering abilities have settled. It is only the sheer potency of the book magic powering the Quip that allowed my clients to see the charac-ters I was bringing onboard. But I quickly realized that I could take people into books anyway—just as you can bookwander with a friend you are touching, it works much the same with a non-bookwanderer. But, of course, you can't take people inside a book without any sort of explanation—it isn't as easy as that.

"This is when I came into contact with the Alchemist—I

won't say I was fortunate, but perhaps some dark stars aligned somewhere. You are perhaps surprised to have heard that Horatio was not the first member of the Bolt family to encounter him. At the time I supposed it was chance, but I now believe that his experiments with book magic led him to me, that my work had caught his attention. Perhaps I should have been warier of his interest in the Quip, but he offered me a way to fulfill my customers' desires. He created a potion for me, one that guests took with their tea on the Quip, and it made their awareness a little . . . fuzzy round the edges. He tried to promise me it was brewed from all-natural ingredients that were just applied ingeniously, but he quickly realized that I was not too fussy about the specifics, as long as the potion didn't cause any lasting harm. I was able to carry on as I had planned. I could take non-bookwanderers anywhere they wanted to go, and they would come back and not quite understand what had happened.

"It *didn't* do them any harm, I don't think, but I soon noticed that people were getting addicted to the feeling it gave them—not the potion, but the sensation of bookwandering itself. They couldn't remember much except that they'd had the most incredible experience and wanted more. I think the general assumption was that they'd taken some sort of hallucinatory drug, and I never let them think otherwise. It's not that far from the truth."

Milo felt winded by all the information, and the more his grandmother spoke of the Alchemist, the more uncomfortable he felt learning it without Alessia. She deserved to hear this about her father at the same time.

"Maybe . . ." he started, breaking Lina's focus. "Maybe we could go down to the library and you could tell me the rest of the story with Rosa and Alessia? I think Alessia should hear this from you."

"You said she knew what her father was like," Lina said.

"Yes, but this isn't for me to hear before her," Milo insisted. "Rosa said to ask you to show me the library when we were ready."

"If that's what you want," Lina said, shrugging. "I could do with some tea anyway. Can you help me down the stairs?"

Milo nodded and stood up to offer his support. Lina pulled back the covers and swung herself round to the edge, taking his arm firmly so she could push herself up. She was only the same height as Milo, and very thin; he could feel her fingers holding on to him tightly.

"Grab my shawl for me, please," she said, gesturing at a colorful scarf on a chair.

Milo picked it up with his other hand and helped arrange it around her shoulders. She kept hold of his arm but picked up a carved wooden walking stick, and very slowly they made their way outside, across the bridge, and down the stairs to the next platform.

This was the level of the treehouse that had the biggest structure built round it; a large main cabin circled the central oak, and smaller ones peeled off from it, curling among the other trees. Lina nodded at the door, which Milo pushed open.

At that moment Milo realized he was being held up by Lina as much as he was steadying her, for inside was the most *beautiful* library he had ever seen—the sight of it took his breath away.

It was not the biggest or the grandest library by far, but it was the *loveliest*, and he immediately felt a little safer.

8

A Terrible Accident

The library was built round the oak tree, and a bench piled with cushions curved around the trunk. The floor space wasn't large, but the library stretched upward to a high ceiling, with ladders leading to narrow landings and balconies, and archways that Milo assumed must lead to the smaller cabins he had seen from outside. Sunshine streamed through small windows, and Milo could see strings of fairy lights, as well as lamps poking out at various points for when night fell. Almost every spot was covered in books: books of all sizes and colors on the shelves lining the walls right up to the ceiling; books piled high on desks squeezed into the spaces between those shelves—even books in a wire cage suspended by some kind of rope-and-pulley system hanging from the roof.

Rosa and Alessia were sitting by a small, enclosed wood burner and looked up as Milo and Lina approached, questions written over both their faces. Alessia had her leg propped up

on a stool with a fresh bandage wrapped around her ankle, and there was the smell of lavender and something else Milo couldn't place in the air.

"Milo decided that Miss Alessia should hear the story too," Lina said abruptly. "Given that it concerns her father."

Alessia glanced at Milo. He wished he could give her a more reassuring look, but he wasn't sure how she would feel after hearing about this extra layer to the Alchemist's schemes and cruelty.

"Shall I make us some tea?" Rosa said a little warily, trying to read the relationship between Lina and Milo.

"Yes, please," Lina said, settling herself by the wood burner. "I can fill Miss della Porta in on my past dealings with her father."

"I'll be as quick as I can," Rosa said to Milo as she jumped up. "The kitchen is just below us. Lina and I drink green tea mainly, but we have all sorts—what can I get you, Milo? Alessia, would you like a hot chocolate?"

"Yes, please," she said.

"Me too, please," Milo said. He wasn't sure if he liked green tea, and he needed something comforting.

As they waited for Rosa, Lina repeated the last part of her story for Alessia, who kept her head high and her face stoic as she took in the details of the drugged potions. Soon Rosa pushed open the library door with her back and carefully carried a tray toward them.

Rosa herself was still an unknown quantity, Milo reminded himself, however comfortable he felt in her library. From the way the Alchemist and even Horatio talked about her, he had been expecting someone considerably more intimidating. He didn't quite understand how this friendly, warm woman with her cozy treehouse library could be anyone's archnemesis. She didn't seem dangerous at all, and was much nicer than her blunt letter to Horatio implied.

Rosa set the tray down on the table between the sofas and handed two chunky mugs full of hot chocolate to Alessia and Milo. A blue-and-white-patterned teapot sat brewing something that smelled fresh and appealing, and a small plate was heaped with crumbly shortbread. Milo realized as he bit into the biscuit quite how hungry he was. Once everyone had a drink and a biscuit, Rosa looked at Lina. "Are you ready to keep going with your story?"

"I am," Lina replied, putting her cup down and drawing her shawl around her tightly.

"So, the Alchemist and I worked together for years and years, and by this time I'd had my twins, Horatio and your father, Asher. Your father was conflicted about the services offered on the Quip from the moment he understood what we did, even though I kept many of the details away from the boys. He begged me to let him go to a regular boarding school, but I didn't want him so far away.

"Then, when he was eighteen, he left and went to work in

a bookshop, where he met your mother, Saira. We stayed in touch, despite his misgivings about what I did. Your parents were always content to live in the real world, bookwandering only for their own pleasure. But once you were born, Milo, they came for trips on the Quip a little more regularly so I could spend time with you. And so your uncle Horatio could get to know you as well, of course. Horatio always had a more . . . *holistic* understanding of our business. He could be flexible in terms of right and wrong, and we made a good team for a long time.

"But, on one such visit, when you were still a baby, Milo, I fixed on the idea of using *The Wizard of Oz* for my next adventure. The Alchemist had long said it would make an ideal destination, and when I mentioned the family was visiting it was his suggestion to go on the Wizard's hot-air balloon. Rosa has since told me more about his particular relationship with that book, but I was none the wiser at the time, and there seemed nothing suspicious in his plan; it's a popular book after all. I wish the Alchemist had told me more. At the time, I sometimes wondered if he was hoping I might be his protégée, that he would be able to share more of his secrets and research with me . . .

"Anyway, we near the end of it all now. Once the idea was there for the hot-air balloon trip, I was set on it. Two birds with one stone: a chance for a family day trip and the opportunity to scope out Oz for my customers. We were all supposed to go together, but as we were getting ready to leave I received a letter from the British Underlibrary saying they had been made aware of what I was doing. They seemed to think they had some jurisdiction over me, despite the fact I was registered with no Underlibrary and have no passport from any country. I was asked to report to London to answer for taking non-bookwanderers into books. I didn't tell Asher about it; he was such a rule-follower and it would have worried him, but I showed Horatio. I had no desire to go to London—I did not want them to find some means of curtailing my freedoms—so I told Horatio that I needed some time to think, but that you should all still go to Oz.

"I thought you could all have a nice day and that I could come up with the best way to evade the Underlibrary by the time you got back. But the next thing I knew, Horatio was staggering back onto the Quip, completely on his own, covered in blood and weeping. He could barely get his words out—he was in a horrible state—but he told me there'd been a terrible accident and that I had to go right that moment or my life would be in danger. He was so distressed; he kept saying that everyone was dead, that he'd done what he had to, and that if the Underlibrary found out my plans had caused their deaths, I would be imprisoned somewhere. He insisted that I hand over the Driver's whistle, and he then took the Quip straight to Northumberland, where he left me at Asher and Saira's empty house. I assume he must have hidden you somewhere and brought you back to the

Quip after I'd gone, as that was the last time I saw him for a very long while."

Lina looked up in the hush that followed her story.

"So, you see, Milo, I believed you to be dead for a long time," she said. "And it would be an insult to pretend that my actions did not lead up to the events of that horrible day, but the true blame lies in Venice, with the Alchemist."

9

One Dark and Stormy Night

Milo sat in shocked silence. It was so much to take in. He glanced at Alessia, who looked troubled. Rosa caught his eye, and for a second he thought she was going to move closer and give him a hug—he was relieved when she didn't. Lina didn't seem particularly sorry or embarrassed by the story she'd told, just worn out.

"How did you end up here at the treehouse?" was the question Milo ended up asking first.

"It was a while before Lina found her way to me," Rosa answered. "I was aware of the Quip, but of course it operates very much off the beaten track, as it were, and I had just heard rumors. Most people had never met the Bolt family, although stories circulated, and I heard gossip that something had gone horribly wrong. Horatio did a significantly better job keeping his enterprises private than Lina—working for a very exclusive client list, and only allowing the right, or rather the *wrong*, people to know he was available for book-smuggling work, as I'm sure you're aware, Milo. I do wish he was here to fill in some of the gaps we have."

Milo nodded. He was more than familiar with his uncle's extreme discreetness.

"He managed to stay off the Underlibrary's radar for the most part," Rosa continued. "And so, once I knew of his activities, I kept an eye on him by becoming his client—although I would be lying if I said the books and manuscripts he's acquired for me haven't also been of great use. He really is very good at finding the most obscure and dangerous things, books that I previously thought only existed in myth.

"But I only met Lina when Horatio turned up here one dark and stormy night, distressed and suspicious. He said he had no idea what to do, and that I was the only one who could help. We talked and I got a little more information about the Alchemist out of him. He calmed down, and we realized that for the moment our goals aligned—and more importantly, that our skills when put together might be enough to stop the Alchemist's power from expanding. As part of that conversation, he also told me about Lina and her tenure as the Quip's Driver, as well as the accident and the need to hide her from both the Alchemist and the Underlibrary. And so I offered to have her here while Horatio and I worked together."

"To keep me prisoner more like," Lina said, and Milo couldn't quite tell how serious she was being.

"It seems to me that you are very lucky to be in such a nice prison," Alessia said fiercely, without the same doubt. Lina only gave a sardonic snort of laughter and lay back against her chair, closing her eyes.

"But all this time I never knew you existed, Milo," Rosa went on, ignoring Lina and Alessia. "Your uncle is a complicated and flawed man, but he kept you hidden away from the Alchemist's eyes so successfully that no one, including your grandmother, knew you were still alive until quite recently. I only suspected in the spring, after I heard stories from the Underlibrary of a book smuggler turning up with a boy in tow. Put together with what I knew of Lina's family, I had asked Horatio, and he had been shifty enough for me to understand who you were. He wouldn't confirm anything, but I assumed it was to do with the Alchemist of course."

"I'm sorry," Alessia said to Milo after Rosa had finished speaking.

"For what?" Milo said, confused.

"Well, it is clear to me that my father is responsible for the death of your parents," she said with a wobbly voice. "And not just by suggesting the trip to Oz. You know how much control he has over that book; I think he was intending for all your family to die that day so that he could take the Quip."

Milo nodded. It was naive to think anything else.

"So why are you apologizing?" he said.

Alessia looked up questioningly.

"What was it you told me about not apologizing for things that aren't our fault?" Milo said as he gave Alessia's hand a small squeeze.

"I hope you won't mind if I comment, Alessia," Rosa added gently. "But for anyone to expect a child of your age to do anything to stop their own father would be cruel and unfair in my opinion. And that doesn't even take into account that you clearly have done a great deal of good by helping Milo escape from Venice—not to mention the useful information you've evidently learned and absorbed. It's a very difficult thing to stand up to our families when we believe them to be wrong, and it sounds to me like you've been incredibly brave."

Alessia gave her a small and tearful smile.

"My question is," said Milo to Alessia, "why didn't your father just kill Horatio when he had the chance?"

"He has never liked to get his hands dirty," Alessia said. "He hires people to do that sort of thing. I guess that's why he wrote up the contract, especially if he believed your uncle was the last member of your family. He was happy to wait a little longer and use your uncle's services in the meantime, and he also needed—"

"I'm sorry to interrupt again," Rosa said. "I'm having to do some catching up here. Firstly, I am convinced Horatio is more deeply involved than we realize. I am sure there is a reason he is still alive. But more pressingly—what contract are you talking about?"

Milo looked up to see that Lina's eyes had opened just a little, and even though she was still lying back as if resting, her body was tense, betraying the keen attention she was paying to the conversation. Given everything that Lina had told them, surely Milo could answer—despite Rosa's own warnings about mentioning the Quip.

"Horatio signed a contract saying that as he had no living relatives, the Quip would go to the Alchemist upon his death," Milo said slowly. "Which obviously isn't true. I'm not even sure that's how the Quip's magic works. But you were working with Horatio—he didn't tell you?"

"I don't think it will come as any surprise to you that your uncle keeps his cards close to his chest, which is especially frustrating now that he is unconscious," Rosa said. "I was under no illusions that he was telling me everything, and I suspected he was trying to pull off some other arrangement with the Alchemist. Of course I had no idea that protecting you, Milo, was also something he was trying to juggle. And now that he himself has been poisoned by the Alchemist, I can't connect the dots. But you have a cure, you say?"

"Something like that," Alessia replied. "It's more of a *recipe* for a cure. We need your help."

"Sounds like I should take a look then," Rosa said. "Because it is imperative we have Horatio awake as quickly as possible. Shall the three of us have some lunch and see what we can do? Lina, I'll bring something up for you later if you're hungry."

"Thank you," Lina said. "I have plenty to think about in the meantime."

The three of them made their way down the stairs to the lowest level of the treehouse. Milo felt a little dazed; he wanted time to grieve his parents, having found out more about what had happened to them, but his brain was too busy worrying about Lina's manner and motivations, and the time pressure to cure Horatio. He knew it probably wasn't a great idea to shove all thought of his parents to the back of his mind for now, but he had no better plan. There was barely enough space there already to process having a grandmother with a very casual approach to drugging people and an unnerving admiration for the Alchemist's work. He had assumed she was being kept safe here, but he now realized that there was a lot being kept safe *from* her as well. An image of Tilly's grandmother flashed across his brain: Elsie at Pages & Co., taking care of everyone, running the bookshop and loving Tilly so very much.

The key thing, he reminded himself, was that they knew more than they had this morning. They had found an ally in Rosa, as far as they could tell, and she seemed confident she could help with the cure. Lina was . . . not quite what he had hoped for, no, but Alessia had also seemed spiky and deceptive only a day ago, and she was rapidly becoming the person he trusted most in the world. When it came to his uncle, it was hard to know what to think—there were pieces of this story only Horatio was going to be able to give them. And so, the only way to get them was to work out the recipe.

The kitchen cabin was small, cozy, and smelled amazing. It was lined with cupboards, a red fridge, and matching oven. Round windows were open to let in the sound of the lapping waters of the lake and birdsong, and a radio was perched on a shelf playing gentle piano music. A wooden table was snug against the wall, with four stools tucked beneath it. Rosa went over to the stovetop and checked under the lid of a shiny blue pot before turning the gas on.

"Parsnip soup okay?" she asked, and Milo and Alessia nodded eagerly. Rosa busied around the kitchen, insisting that they sit down and rest, that she didn't need any help. A warm loaf of crusty bread was produced from the oven and put on the table with a dish of golden butter and a block of crumbly cheese. Colorful, mismatched bowls, cutlery, and glasses emerged from

the various cupboards, and before long the three of them were sitting down with steaming bowls of soup.

"How's your ankle feeling now?" Rosa asked Alessia.

"Much better actually," Alessia remarked in surprise. "I had forgotten about it, which has to be a good sign. That ointment must be magic."

"Just the magic of various herbs and plants." Rosa smiled. "I'm glad it's making a difference."

And for the first time in a while, Milo thought that maybe everything would work out okay in the end. Someone who could make soup this good would surely be able to help them.

10

A Little More Whimsical
Than I Was Expecting

After they'd eaten, Rosa made more tea. Milo tried the green tea this time and found it unusual but refreshing. It was what he imagined drinking grass might be like—if it were very fancy grass. He decided he quite enjoyed it.

"Milo," Rosa said. "I'm here if you have questions about Lina, which I'm sure you do. But shall we take a look at the recipe now and see what we can do to help Horatio? So let's have a glance at the ingredients, see what we're working with, and then I'd be very grateful if you would fetch the poison compendium for me."

"Of course," Milo said gratefully.

Alessia pulled out her tatty notebook and passed it to Rosa, who weighted it down so that the three of them could see the list of ingredients copied in haste in Alessia's slightly messy handwriting from her father's study.

Cure for poison he uses on book Alessia had written at the top of the page. Milo saw that there was a question mark at the end of the title that had since been scribbled out.

It went on:

1. *Death made into life, to respect the work of the poison*
2. *A token of unnatural nature, to honor the power of the imagination*
3. *Something stolen honestly, to signify the gift of the cure*
4. *Something lost properly, for the time taken*
5. *An impossibility, to break the limbo they are held in*
6. *Ground ginger root, to soothe the patient on awakening*
7. *A seventh, for completeness: the record of the reader, for intent*

To brew, distill all ingredients apart from the last over flames with the fifth element. When transformed, add the record of the reader to ensure specificity. Administer to the patient within seven hours of adding the record.

"Right then," Rosa said. "This is, I'll admit, a little more . . . whimsical than I was expecting."

"Yes," said Milo slowly. "When you said you weren't sure

what some of the ingredients were, I just thought you meant they were things you hadn't heard of, not literal riddles."

"Oh, my father sees himself as having poetic flair," Alessia said grimly. "He thinks it speaks to how clever he is, and why he should be ruling the world. He hates most modern leaders because he thinks you need—what does he say?—*an artist's soul* to manage power. I guess it also makes it pretty difficult for anyone else to interpret and make the cure."

"But you said you knew what some of this meant," Milo prompted Alessia.

"I'm fairly sure that a lot of the items come from books—that they have to be made of imagination," she said. "I don't know *how* he gets things out of books, or how he turns them into a cure, though."

"I may be able to help on that front," Rosa said. "Once we understand what we need and where to get it. Do you have any other pointers?"

"Only that he would get at least one of these ingredients from an Underlibrary—he used to go to the one in Rome quite often. He definitely has spies or undercover librarians there."

Rosa peered at the list.

"This fourth item," she said, pointing. "I know you had to write this very quickly—do you think you might have copied it down wrong? Did you translate this from Italian? Should it be something from lost *property*? Not something lost *properly*?"

"No, he often writes in English," Alessia said. "He says

that he thinks in English and Italian all at the same time, some-times other languages too. But I might have written it wrong, I *was* going fast; that's why it's so messy. It could easily be 'lost property'—that makes more sense."

"In which case I think I know what it is," Rosa said. "Every Underlibrary has a Lost Property Office. You know how the Endpapers function as a sort of bumper for stories and char-acters, to keep everything in its right place or catch things that have gone wrong?"

"Yes," Milo said. "Tilly can use them to travel to the Underlibraries too—because she's half-fictional. You know about Tilly . . . right?" Milo realized he was assuming that Rosa knew almost everything, given her obvious power and connections.

"I do, a little," Rosa confirmed. "It is not so secret that she is half-fictional anymore; neither is what she did at the Underlibrary to free the Source Editions. That is interesting about her ability to travel via the Endpapers." Although even the way she said the last part made Milo think that perhaps she already knew about that too.

"We must talk more about Tilly and how she's doing once we've tackled this cure," Rosa went on. "But back to the Lost Property Offices at the Underlibraries. As far as I understand it, they deal with any bookwanderers who get lost in the Endpapers, and perhaps they handle objects too; I have never visited one myself. Alessia, I imagine your father could easily lay his hands on something there. We, however, might have a little more trouble."

"If we're going to the British Underlibrary, I'm sure Tilly could help," Milo said. "Then you can talk to her directly. And Amelia Whisper might too—she's in charge of the British Underlibrary at the moment and knows what's going on. Maybe she'd let us have something small."

"Perfect," Rosa said. "I'm very keen to make sure Tilly and Pages & Co. are safe too, so we can hopefully tick both things off at the same time. That's one ingredient down, then—what else is on the list?"

"Ginger," Alessia answered. "But I know what that is, obviously."

"Yes, wonderful, another thing easily sorted," Rosa said. "I have plenty of ginger here."

"We know what the record of a reader is too," Milo said. "And we had Horatio's, from the Archive, but . . . well, the Records have gone all blurry and messy. You can't read them. We can show you—they're on the Quip."

"As you mention it, it is perhaps now a good time for you to bring the Quip a little closer, and for you to show me the poison compendium?" Rosa asked. "I have hopes it might help me stop the Alchemist completely, but I also have a whisper of an idea for one of the cure ingredients, and I wonder if the compendium will contain something we can use. Let's start there while we think on the more esoteric items."

"Esoteric?" Alessia queried.

"It means something hard to understand, or something

only people with a very particular knowledge base will be able to interpret," Rosa said. "I'm glad you asked. I'm a big believer in asking the meaning of words you don't know."

Alessia glowed at the compliment.

"I'm cautiously optimistic we'll be able to puzzle this through, Milo," Rosa said. "I think between the three of us we stand a pretty good chance."

"Really?" Milo asked, feeling the glimmer of hope awaken again.

"We'll give it our best shot," Rosa said. "Everything we know about the Alchemist and how he operates helps us understand how to stop him. Even getting a sense for how he builds his potions and poisons helps us see his workings, shows us his weaknesses—not that having a flair for the dramatic is a weakness. But I wonder if that's something we might be able to use against him. Now, would you show me the Quip, and we can start collecting these ingredients?"

11 ★

Not Exactly an Ordinary Greenhouse

As the three of them walked back toward the sycamore tree, Rosa told them a little more about her work.

"I'll take you up to the greenhouse once we have the poison cabinet," she said. "It's my favorite spot in the tree-house, apart from the library perhaps. So, how did Horatio get the compendium out of Oz in the end?"

"He didn't," Milo explained. "Tilly and I did."

"Well, that's very impressive," Rosa said. "You've learned some tricks from your uncle, clearly."

"Not really," Milo said, unsure how he felt being too closely compared to Horatio. "It was because of Tilly—she can take things out of books, it's another way her bookwandering is unusual. And it's why the Alchemist thinks that Tilly is the Anonymous Reader."

Rosa stopped walking abruptly. "What did you say?" she

asked sharply. And for a fraction of a second, Milo saw why someone might be scared of her.

"Th—the Alchemist thinks Tilly is the Anonymous Reader."

Rosa seemed to be collecting herself. "That's what I thought. My apologies, I was not expecting to hear that term from you," she said. "This is unsettling news. Is there anything else he said on the subject?"

"Just that he believes it's her, and, well, that he wants her to get *The Book of Books* for him. He thinks it's here . . ."

"Is it here?" Alessia asked curiously.

"No," Rosa said after a pause. "But I have no reason not to trust you with the information that I am its guardian—and the only person who knows where it truly is hidden. It must not fall into his hands. Has he asked Tilly to come and get it? Threatened her, no doubt?"

"He tried to make a deal with Tilly," Milo explained. "This was obviously before we all ran away, so he didn't know that Alessia had stolen the cure or the recipe. He was going to trade Tilly's grandfather's health for the Book. He'll have noticed by now we took the cure, but I don't know how long it'll take him to realize we know how to complete it too."

"The last we heard from him was the note he sent via the Quip to Tilly," Alessia went on. "Where he said again that he would swap the Book for the cure for Archie. Once he knows that Tilly's grandad is awake and he doesn't have that leverage, I'm not sure what he'll do."

"And Tilly is safely at home at Pages & Co. right now?" Rosa asked.

"Yes," Milo said. "But if we stick to the plan to get her help at the Underlibrary, you can ask her more about this very soon."

"Right then, all the more reason to get this cure started," Rosa said.

They reached the Quip quickly, and Rosa looked at the train in admiration.

"Well, isn't she beautiful?" she said, putting a hand on the Quip's shiny exterior.

"Come in," Milo said. As he opened the door with Rosa watching, his heart felt full, and he didn't fumble with the key. He was proud, he realized—an unfamiliar sensation for him. "Should we get the train back to the treehouse first, before we show you the Records and the poison cabinet?" he asked, pulling the Driver's whistle out on the chain that he always wore round his neck.

"That's a good idea," Rosa agreed. "I think putting her by the lake makes sense, if that's okay with you?"

Milo liked very much that Rosa didn't ask him about how the whistle and the Quip worked; she seemed simply content to trust him to get on with it. She had a way of appearing entirely at peace with herself wherever she was, and she looked around the carriage curiously but didn't touch anything.

He blew the whistle and imagined the lakeside as clearly as he could. Every time he drove the Quip, it felt a little more natural. Like a key catching the right spot in a lock so it opens a door, his mind found exactly the right place to clearly tell the Quip where he wanted to go, and he felt confident that it understood.

It took mere moments to get the Quip back to the tree-house, and they parked it among the trees by the lake. Milo was glad they could keep it close.

"Do you have some night things and clothes you could bring?" Rosa suggested. "I think you'll probably end up staying the night here, and while I could rustle some up, I'm sure you'll be more comfortable in your own."

"I just have what I brought with me in my rucksack from Venice," Alessia said. "But it's enough for now."

"I'll go grab some stuff from my carriage," Milo said, and ran along the train to his cozy room. There he gathered up clean bits and pieces as quickly as he could.

When he returned to the office, Alessia was picking up the blurry Records, getting ready to go. She pointed at Horatio's coded notebooks, and Milo gave a nod to signify she should bring them, hoping Rosa might be able to work out the code they were written in. Alessia gathered them up too, while Milo hoisted his bag onto his back and then lifted the poison compendium from the desk.

"This is yours," he said, giving it to Rosa before opening the door to the Quip.

"Thank you," she said. "I can't tell you how impressed I am

that you and Tilly managed to find it and get it out—clearly you two and Alessia make for quite the ingenious trio."

"Are you okay carrying it?" Milo asked politely. "It's quite delicate."

"I am, thank you," Rosa said, watching her step as she stepped down from the train. "I'm going to take this straight to my greenhouse and have a look, if you'd like to come too? It's where I do most of my work as a botanist. Though, of course, many of my experiments and inventions have at least a little touch of book magic to them, so it's not exactly an *ordinary* greenhouse."

Both Milo and Alessia nodded eagerly. Milo had almost forgotten, now that he thought of her as *Rosa*, that this was the Botanist they had heard about, the great enemy of the Alchemist, and he was curious to see where she did . . . well, whatever it was she did. If it was enough to threaten the Alchemist, it had to be interesting. He was fascinated that someone could be so powerful while also so kind.

Back at the treehouse, they headed up the stairs right to the top level, where a platform had been built among the highest branches and leaves. And on the platform was a glass greenhouse, circular like many of the other cabins.

"Could you get the door for me, please, Milo?" Rosa asked, her hands full with the poison compendium. "It's not locked."

Milo reached out and took hold of the ornate metal handle and opened the door, before standing back to let Rosa lead the way.

12

Riddles

As he took in the space around him, Milo thought to himself that each bit of the treehouse was more amazing and beautiful than the last.

A wooden table stood in the center of the room, piled high with notebooks, drawings, and reference texts, some open to intricate drawings of plants and trees. Over their heads were long ropes of cord hung with dried herbs and flowers, and shelves of terra-cotta plant pots lined one of the glass walls. A cabinet on the far side was full of small labeled bottles, too far away to read. One nook housed a blackboard covered in notes and diagrams, a small wood-burning stove, and a well-worn, squishy red armchair. To Milo, the place felt overwhelmingly peaceful, despite the clutter and busyness.

"Welcome to my greenhouse!" Rosa said cheerfully. "It's more my study, really. You can see I do grow some bits and pieces here, but it's where I do all my work and my research."

"I'm still not sure I quite understand what your work is, exactly," Alessia said bluntly. Milo's first instinct was to be embarrassed by her straightforward question, but he was always glad she asked these things.

"Well," Rosa said, setting down the poison compendium on the table. "If your father's work is at the intersection of book magic and science, perhaps the easiest answer is that mine is

at the midpoint between book magic and nature. Now, that's a simplistic explanation, as I use a lot of science, and he clearly respects the natural world. But with regard to book magic and imagination in particular, he is trying to manipulate and *change* what exists, and I am looking to preserve and protect it."

"I'm sorry if this is a rude question," Milo said, "but why? You seem very . . . involved in everything to do with bookwandering. You know a lot of stuff that not many people know. How did you end up being the guardian of *The Book of Books*?"

"That's an excellent question," Rosa said. "And I don't have an official job title; it's not like at the Underlibraries where everything is ordered and formal. My role is inherited; it passed down to me from my mother, who taught me what I needed to know to keep the Book safe from anyone who would seek to use it to exert too much power over bookwandering. So, shall we see what we can find in this cabinet? I have high hopes there may be something here that can help us against the Alchemist."

"And you think there might be something that will help with the antidote as well?" Milo asked. "Something that might fit one of the riddles?"

"It's a possibility," Rosa said. "But that would be a bonus— I've been trying to get hold of this for a while now."

"What is it that you're hoping to find?" Alessia asked as Rosa unhooked the clasps that kept the box together.

"There is a substance in Norse mythology called *eitr*," Rosa said. "It is known as something that can both begin and end life. It's the source of all life, but can also poison the gods themselves. In fact, the word for poison in Icelandic is *eitur*, from that very substance. And I wonder if it might work for the first ingredient. Indeed, perhaps it was what the Alchemist himself used to make the poison. *Death made into life*. Eitr is a life-giving poison; it seems to fit.

"But crucially eitr might also hold the key to separating the Alchemist from his unnatural control of book magic. I know he must be drawing power from somewhere very potent, and I had suspected that it might be *The Wizard of Oz* from what Lina told me of the balloon accident, but now I *know* this is true. Succeeding in this would not necessarily defeat him, but I believe it would lessen his power significantly, and give us a chance to stop him for good. Which is why I asked Horatio to try and find this compendium for me."

"So, is it in there?" Alessia interrupted impatiently. "This eitr stuff?"

Rosa turned her attention to the worn labels on the drawers and bottles in the cabinet. As she read the scrawled handwriting and opened the tiny compartments, sniffing at what was inside, she got more and more frantic. She let empty drawers drop to the table as she looked for false backs or bottoms.

Soon all that was left was one empty bottle, with no label at all. Rosa abandoned it on the table and took a deep breath.

"Is . . . is it not there?" Milo asked nervously.

"It would seem not," Rosa said, wiping her hand across her forehead.

"Is this anything?" Alessia asked, showing them the bottom of the unlabeled bottle. On the glass was a very small, crudely etched symbol. It looked a bit like a wonky capital "F," as the horizontal lines were at an angle.

Rosa peered intently at it.

"It's a kind of rune, I think," she said. "I have no idea what it means, but I don't think it's too big of a leap to hope it symbolizes eitr in some way, or some concoction the Alchemist has made with it. It certainly looks Norse; we'll have to look it up. But regardless, it's completely empty." She shook the bottle to make sure, and it was bone-dry.

"But if that rune does mean eitr, then you were right that my father at least had or used some in the past?" Alessia said, trying to be positive. "Maybe we can bookwander with Tilly into a myth and go and get some more!"

"Perhaps," Rosa said, sitting down heavily in disappointment.

"I wonder if there's anything in my uncle's notebooks," Milo suggested, pulling them out and passing them to Rosa. "They're in code, just so you're prepared, and we couldn't make any sense of them."

"Your uncle and his obsessive secrets," Rosa sighed as she took them. "Thank you for sharing these with me, though." She flicked through the pages and gave another deep sigh. "I'm going to need some time with these," she said. "Our immediate problem is what to use for your cure if we can't use this. *Death made into life, to respect the work of the poison* was written in your ingredients, but we don't want to be meddling with anything too dark if we can help it."

"What about a vampire?" Alessia suggested. "There's a few vampire novels I'd love to bookwander into."

"While it fits the criteria, I'm not sure it's a good idea to try and remove any pieces of a vampire," Rosa said.

"That's fair." Alessia nodded. "Although I think it's a strong backup option."

"I have an idea," Milo said quietly. Rosa and Alessia turned to him expectantly. "This might not be a *good* idea, so just ignore me if I'm wrong, but don't gardens come back to life every spring?"

"Oh, that's interesting," Rosa said. "I know just the place we can go. Have either of you read *The Secret Garden*?"

13

Do You Believe in Magic?

After picking up a full backpack from the greenhouse table, Rosa led the two children back down to the library to find a copy of *The Secret Garden* by Frances Hodgson Burnett. Both of them had heard of it, but neither had read it before. Rosa quickly pulled a copy off the shelf and passed it to Alessia.

"Could you turn to chapter eight, please?" she said. "I'm just going to find some more suitable clothes." In one nook in the library was what Milo could only describe as a dressing-up box. It was jam-packed with all sorts of clothes, from ball-gowns to trench coats to old-fashioned dresses. Rosa rooted around in it and pulled out an assortment of knitwear, hats, and scarves. "Find something that fits—it'll be a bit nippy in Yorkshire," she said. Milo yanked on a gray flat cap and wrapped a colorful knitted scarf round his neck. Alessia somehow managed to find a matching navy-blue bobble hat, scarf, and gloves, which she made look very chic.

"Okay, ready? Is your ankle going to be all right?" Rosa said to Alessia, who gave a thumbs-up. She handed the book to Rosa, who turned one page back, ran a finger down the paper, and alighted on the sentence she was looking for. She held her arm out for Milo to tuck his hand into, and Alessia took hold of Milo's other hand. Rosa started to read.

"Mary skipped round all the gardens and round the orchard, resting every few minutes. At length she went to her own special walk and made up her mind to try if she could skip the whole length of it. It was a good long skip and she began slowly, but before she had gone half-way down the path she was so hot and breathless that she was obliged to stop. She did not mind much, because she had already counted up to thirty. She stopped with a little laugh of pleasure, and there, lo and behold, was the robin swaying on a long branch of ivy."

The first thing Milo became aware of was the cold, and he was very glad of the hat and scarf Rosa had given him. They were standing at the edge of an orchard in winter; trees were trained against the walls—bare, spindly lines of them. The grass was brown and dead, and the whole place felt damp and miserable. Rosa put a finger to her lips and gestured to the long avenue that lay ahead of them. Milo and Alessia quietly followed her out of

the orchard, onto the path, which
was bordered by empty flower
beds and ivy-draped walls. A
little way down was a small,
thin girl in a white wool coat
holding a skipping rope. She
was staring in delight up at a
robin perched among the ivy.

"You showed me where the key was yesterday," they heard
her say. "You ought to show me the door today; but I don't
believe you know!" At that the robin flew onto the top of the
wall, singing loudly as if he were showing off. As he flew, the
wind started to pick up, channeled through the walls of the
long avenue, rustling the ivy from side to side. Alessia lifted her
gloved hands to move her long hair from her face, but the tickly
woolly gloves made her wrinkle her nose and then let out a
gigantic sneeze. The girl in the white coat looked up in surprise
and saw the three of them watching her. Her face immediately
dropped, the wonder leaving it abruptly, replaced by suspicion.

"Who are you?" she asked tightly.

"My name is Rosa," Rosa replied, moving a little closer to
the girl. "And this is Milo and Alessia."

"Those are strange names," the girl said. "My name is Mary
Lennox."

"Nice to meet you, Mary," Rosa responded, and Milo offered
a small wave.

"Are you from India?" Mary asked Milo bluntly, taking in his brown skin.

"No, but my family is," Milo said, a little warily.

"I used to live in India," answered Mary. "But then my parents and everyone I knew died, and I was sent here." She said it as though it were a challenge.

"Well, Milo's parents died too, I don't know who my mother is, and my father is a monster, so we all have our burdens," Alessia said sharply.

Mary looked shocked. "How dare you speak to me like that?" she said, her face tightening even more. "I hope you know that these grounds all belong to my uncle. You are either trespassing or most badly behaved servants."

"I'm not a servant!" Alessia said. "Although I suppose we are trespassing," she added thoughtfully.

"We're friends, I promise," Milo said, trying to offset Alessia's bluntness, which was clearly a very bad fit with Mary Lennox's prickliness.

"I don't have any friends," Mary said stiffly.

"He means that we don't intend you any harm," Rosa said. "We didn't want to interrupt you at all."

"What were you doing then?" Mary said suspiciously. "Do you know about the garden? I thought it was a secret."

Milo was curious about the way Mary was dealing with their presence. Usually when you bookwandered, characters very quickly got used to you being there and just accepted you, however unlikely it was. But Mary Lennox was putting up more resistance than usual. She made for an unexpected heroine, Milo thought to himself.

"It is a secret," Rosa reassured Mary. "It's been shut up and locked for years."

"I know," Mary said defensively. "But the robin showed me the key the other day, and I think he was trying to show me the door too before you interrupted. And now he's flown away."

"No, look, he's still here, just watching," Rosa said, pointing up at the robin, who was perched a little farther down the wall with his head cocked to one side, closely observing what was happening beneath him. He chirruped and flew back to them, just as the wind picked up again. It was noticeably stronger than before, buffeting around them, whispering and rustling through the dry flower beds and ivy. And then, all of a sudden, the wind caught hold of the loose ivy trails by Mary, and there, underneath, was the knob of a door.

Mary gasped in delight.

"Do you believe in magic?" she asked the three bookwanderers, and it felt like one of those questions that a lot hinged on. Thankfully, there wasn't a shadow of a doubt for any of them.

"With all my heart," Rosa said, and Mary gave a sharp little nod of acceptance and turned back to the door.

The ivy hung thickly, like a rustling curtain. Mary started to pull it aside, and Milo jumped in to help. Mary didn't say thank you, but she didn't bristle or stop him. He could see that her cheeks were flushed and her hands were shaking with excitement; and the robin was matching that joy, flittering around their hands and singing as if in anticipation of what they were about to find.

"Here!" Mary said after a few moments. She knelt down, and Milo could see an old iron lock level with her eyes. Mary pulled an old key from her coat pocket and slid it into the keyhole. She had to use both hands wrapped tightly around it to get it to turn, but then there was the sound of it scratching round.

Mary checked over her shoulder to see if anyone was coming down the path, and then, breathing quickly, she pushed it open and slipped through. For a second, Milo wondered if she was going to close and lock the door behind her, but then a pale hand emerged across the threshold and beckoned, and Milo, Alessia, and Rosa followed her inside.

"We're here," Mary breathed in wonder. "We're *inside* the secret garden."

14

Imaginationeers

The garden they stood in looked as dead as the orchard outside the wall, but there was something undeniably alive about the feel of the place. Something alive and mysterious and wonderful. The high walls cut it off from the ordered sadness outside, and the cold blue sky was bright above them. There was a wildness in here that felt like . . . Well, it felt like bookwandering, Milo couldn't help but think.

The garden was full of winter; brown and dead. Straggling bushes had sprung up at random, and the walls were covered with thick, bare stems; so many of them they made a kind of woven net of stalks.

"I think these are roses," Mary said, looking at the stalks more closely. "I saw a great many roses in India, so I know about these things. And look, those are roses also. Climbing roses, I should think. They're like a fairy arch." She pointed at one of the most unusual and beautiful things about the garden: delicate brown and gray tendrils that spilled from the branches, creating swaying curtains which covered much of the garden. In another space it might have looked quite sinister, but there was something about the air here that made it strange and lovely instead.

"How still it is," Mary whispered to herself. "How still!" And, indeed, when there were neither footsteps nor voices, there was just the whispering of the climbing rose tendrils, and the chirp of the robin, who had followed them inside.

Mary seemed to have forgotten that she had company, she was so entranced. She began to walk farther from the door, skipping rope hooked over her arm, the robin following her closely. Her footsteps were so soft and quiet that she was like a ghost making her way across the grass. She walked through one of the natural arches that the tendrils made, brushing her hand through them as she went. Milo felt as though he were intruding on something deeply private, and he reminded himself that Mary usually had this moment on her own.

As they watched, she knelt down to examine tiny green sprouts, touching them gently, and then crouching lower to take a great sniff of the earth, looking utterly delighted by it. Before long she'd found a piece of wood that worked well enough as a little trowel and started pulling weeds and dead grass from around the tiny shoots, which were the brightest, greenest things in the garden.

"Shall we leave her to it?" Rosa smiled. "I think we should let her discover things for herself."

"Yes," Milo agreed straightaway. "I feel I shouldn't be here, watching her."

"I don't mind," Alessia said. "But I want to help her. Can we?"

"Not right now," Rosa said. "I think this part is important for Mary to do on her own, and we need to find the right bit of the garden for the cure. But perhaps, once the cure is made and the Alchemist dealt with, we could come back later in the book and she how she's getting on."

Milo and Alessia both agreed they'd very much like to do that.

"So, we need something that was dead and has come to life," Alessia recited. "But the garden doesn't really come back to life, does it? Surely Mary just, what, replants the dead stuff? I don't know much about gardening."

"I think that given your father's style, we could probably use anything growing inside the garden walls," Rosa said. "In the book, the whole garden comes back to life as far as its characters—and its readers—understand, and that's all that matters."

"Do you think we could take something from here for the unnatural nature thing too?" Milo asked.

"I had thought about that as well," answered Rosa. "But two things gave me pause. I am not sure this garden counts as unnatural, apart from its fictional nature, and I also believe the number of ingredients is important. The recipe says seven for completeness. Seven is the number of wholeness, so I think we need seven different components for it to work. For now I think we just need a part of a plant to be our dead thing come back to life."

"Great, so we can just grab something and go!" Alessia said, reaching out to the nearest bush and yanking off a handful of twigs.

"I would prefer something a little more meaningful," Rosa said, looking around. "I wonder if there are any . . . Ah yes, look!" She led them over to a cluster of trees with distinctive trunks; dark knots were visible underneath peeling, papery white bark.

"Birch trees!" Rosa announced. "They symbolize new beginnings and rebirth. Perfect." She reached out and snapped a slender twig off a tree.

"And you're sure it counts?" Milo said anxiously.

"As sure as we're going to be about any of these ingredients," Rosa said gently.

"Apart from the ginger," chimed in Alessia.

"Yes, apart from the ginger," Rosa allowed.

"But how do we get the twig out of the book?" Milo asked. "We don't have Tilly with us."

"Right," Rosa said, taking her backpack off. "Well, as you know, I study book magic. The deep roots of it. Where it comes from, why it works. Why imagination and stories are deep in our bones. They're close to the surface for bookwanderers, but they're in every single person, even if buried very deep or used for terrible purposes. Do you remember what Mary said to us, just before she unlocked the door?"

"She asked if we believed in magic," Alessia said.

"Exactly." Rosa smiled. "If you read the book, she doesn't say that to anyone, as we're not usually here of course. But what she thinks to herself, when the wind blows right at that moment to move the ivy and show her the door, is that it was magic."

"But all books are full of the magic of imagination," Milo said.

"Precisely," Rosa said. "This birch twig is simultaneously real birchwood *and* birchwood made of imagination."

"That's all well and good," Alessia said, "but how do we get it out?"

"I'm coming to that," Rosa said patiently. "My point is that it's all made of imagination, so we need to distill the twig to its purest form. This is where we have to get a little bit creative. As you know, you can't take things that are of Story from a book, but you can take your *own* objects back with you, objects that don't originate here. Thankfully our clothes don't stay behind, for example—or your glasses, Milo. So, we must take the things we are studying and make them into something else. Through a lot of research and trial and error, I realized that by distilling it down to pure imagination using tools we have brought from home, we can create almost a third category. Not entirely of our world, but also no longer of this world, it is its own thing and not bound by the same rules and barriers."

"Okay that's pretty clever," Alessia said admiringly. "I wonder if my father has thought of that."

"I imagine he has," Rosa replied. "He's done such extensive work into book magic, and also how to break its rules—it's perhaps where our work overlaps. Alchemy at its core is about turning things into other things, so I have no doubt he utilizes equivalent techniques—I dread to think what for."

"But why haven't other people thought of this?" Milo said.

"Well, firstly, what use would an item from a story be if you had to turn it into something else?" Rosa asked. "The main reasons someone would want something are that it has sentimental or nostalgic meaning or it is valuable in some way. Neither of those hold if you fundamentally change it, and to remove something from a book you really have to alter it irreversibly—you can't just change its superficial physical appearance. Secondly, as I said, it's taken me years of research to find this process, and I'm not sure it would occur to most bookwanderers to try and create this in-between form, or that they would know how to achieve it. As I'm sure you know, a lot of bookwanderers simply don't understand quite how powerful pure imagination is. It is frustratingly and gloriously malleable."

Rosa was methodically removing items from her backpack and laying them out neatly in front of her as she spoke. She set up a small device that Milo thought looked a little like a wax burner, as it had space for a lit candle underneath it, with a concave dip on top where you could rest something. On this she placed a shallow dish, which Milo initially thought was metal. But on closer inspection he realized he wasn't at all sure what it was made of. It was very fine, and as the sunlight hit the surface, waves of rainbow light refracted around it. The light patterns reminded him of the color of the elixir they had made with Alessia's father's recipe, the one he had used to book-wander without a book and that had allowed Artemis to escape the Archive.

"What's that bowl made of?" he asked curiously.

"Ah, well spotted, Milo," Rosa said. "Remember how I just said the best way to take things from books is to distill them into something else?"

"Is this bowl made of imagination too?"

"Exactly," Rosa said. "I'm not sure I can remember what it started life as. I've had it a very long time now."

"Wow," breathed Milo.

"But, you know, it's not so different from that train of yours," Rosa said. "I don't know its whole history, but I think to be able to do what it does, it must at least have a generous dose of pure imagination in there."

Alessia meanwhile had gone into complete research mode, producing a tiny notebook and pencil from some pocket or other and making notes as Rosa set up and explained things to Milo.

"You two would make excellent Imaginationeers." Rosa grinned.

"It's definitely preferable to my father's alchemy," Alessia said, forehead creased in concentration as she sketched the burner and bowl.

"Is that a real job title?" Milo asked curiously.

"As real as any other," Rosa said. "Guardian of *The Book of Books* and Imaginationeer. What do you think? Sounds quite catchy, I reckon."

Rosa gently placed the birch twig in the shimmering bowl and added a few drops of liquid from a small, stoppered bottle. A familiar smell emanated as it heated.

"Rosemary," Alessia said as she sniffed the air.

"Correct!" said Rosa. "Rosemary has a great many uses, among which is that it is excellent for memory. It's there so the birch remembers its nature. I see you looking a little skeptical, Alessia."

"It's just . . . It's not very scientific, is it?" she admitted.

"No, not particularly," Rosa said. "Science is a wonderful thing, but this is magic. Nature and magic."

"You're asking us to believe that heating this birch with rosemary allows you to change the twig into pure imagination while retaining some of what it represents in the story?" Alessia said.

"Exactly," Rosa replied happily. "You seem to have an excellent grasp of it. Remember," she went on more gently, "we are inside a story; all of this—the garden, Mary, the robin, the ivy—was imagined to life by Frances Hodgson Burnett when she wrote the book and then by us when we read it. You have believed stranger things, I am sure. Now, look."

In the shallow bowl the birch wasn't burning but sparkling and glittering with the same qualities that Milo was used to seeing from the windows of the Quip; the paper-white bark was threaded through with veins of silver. And then, all of a sudden, with a whoosh of sweet-smelling air, the twig gave a little shudder and dissolved away entirely into a *shimmering dust* that looked just like the remnants of the orbs of book magic Milo burned in the Quip's engine. Rosa took a fresh glass bottle and a small funnel from her kit and carefully poured the powder into the bottle before stoppering it tight. She wrote "Birch, *The Secret Garden*" on the bottle and slipped it gently into a pouch in her backpack.

"One ingredient down," Alessia said, satisfied, but before they could say more, Mary Lennox was running over the grass to them.

It was like seeing a different person; her knees and fingernails were muddy, her cheeks were pink, and there was a sparkle in her eyes grown from excitement and fresh air.

"I have been clearing space around all the green shoots I could find," she said. "I forgot that you were here as well, until I smelled something strange and sweet. I plan to continue until I have to go for my midday dinner, and then I'll come back this afternoon." And with that she ran back to another corner of the garden to search for more shoots of life to help grow.

"I should read this book, I think," Milo said. "I want to know how it all turns out."

"We may be able to visit later," Rosa said. "Although, just so you know, if you do pick it up, it was written over a hundred years ago, when many people had very different ideas and understandings about people different from them, some of which we now know to be wrong. And Mary as a character grows up in India when it was under British colonial rule and has inherited some of their damaging beliefs. I haven't read it cover to cover in a while, but there might be some lines in there that make you feel uncomfortable or upset, both of you. If you read it while you're at the treehouse, then do let me know if you want some more context. I'm sure Tilly's grandparents would also have some interesting things to say about it, and other books written at the same time."

"Okay," Milo said quietly, not quite sure how to respond. He wished he could talk to someone in his family about their past, but Horatio was unconscious, and Lina . . . Well, he wasn't sure he trusted Lina's take on anything.

"Are you ready to get going?" Rosa said gently. "We have several more ingredient clues to decipher and find, after all. Alessia, would you like to read us out?" She passed the book to Alessia, who turned to the last page as the three of them linked arms again.

"*Across the lawn came the Master of Misselthwaite and he looked as many of them had never seen him . . .*" Alessia read, and the last sentence of the book was lost to Milo's ears as

a great gust of wind blew up, just as it had on the

path outside the garden, rustling and swishing

all the climbing rose tendrils and dried brushes.

As the garden started to dissolve around them, Milo saw Mary look up, watching them go with her homemade trowel in her hand, still clearing space for the tiny shoots to keep growing.

15

The Roots of the World

The greenhouse reappeared around them, and the three of them arrived safely back in the treehouse. The first thing Rosa did was take the bottle out of her backpack and place it carefully on the table in front of them.

"I usually store everything I take from books over there with my ingredients," Rosa said, gesturing to the cabinet filled with bottles. "But let's keep this out; hopefully we'll be needing it to make the cure very soon."

"Is everything in the cabinet made of book magic of some kind then?" Alessia asked.

"A fair amount of it," Rosa said. "But there are some more conventional ingredients in there too. Quite a lot of the stuff up here in the greenhouse is just for regular botany—nothing to do with book magic."

"Were you a normal botanist first?" Milo asked, digging for details.

"Oh no." She smiled. "The book magic definitely came first. I always knew I would inherit guardianship of *The Book of Books* from my mother, and so I didn't prepare for anything else. But that included studying a lot of folklore: ancient stories that have lasted for so long and been repurposed so many times. Through that I became fascinated by how plants and the natural world are used by humans in storytelling, and also in medicine and homes and our lives generally. It's what got me onto this idea that maybe it's all connected, the things that exist deep inside us. Imagination is in our bones and in the roots of the world.

"Ideally, my role would have been as more of an observer, a protector from afar, but the Alchemist has been slowly shifting the calibration of imagination in this world. Everything is being pushed out of sync as he tries to change the fundamental rules of imagination and magic. There have always been people who have meddled, and he's taking it to an extreme. I don't think there's any way to stop him without gaining a greater understanding of what he is doing and how he is manipulating book magic so potently. Yet he has more schemes and plans in motion than I realized; I knew your uncle for years and had no idea he had entered into this secret agreement with the Alchemist in an attempt to keep you and the Quip as safe as possible. At least Horatio's being looked after at Pages & Co. currently. And we've taken our first step to curing him."

"Yes," Milo agreed, but he started to feel panicky as he

thought about his uncle at the bookshop. His breathing sped up and his heart fluttered. "I just left him there, and I didn't even ask permission," he said, worrying. "They must think I'm a horrible person, that I'm just like Horatio, using people when I need them."

"I don't think anyone who has met you even for the briefest moment would think that you were like your uncle," Rosa said. "But if you didn't tell them you were going . . ."

"We did leave a note," Alessia pointed out. "We said we were going to try and find the cure."

"Did you say you were coming here?" Rosa asked.

"We said we were going to try and find you," Alessia said. "But we didn't exactly know where you were."

"And do Tilly and her family have a way of keeping in touch with you?" Rosa asked. "They do know how to reach the Quip, I'm assuming?"

"Yes," Milo said. "I'd forgotten; I should go and check the postbox." He turned to Alessia. "Your father might have been in touch again too, since his last letter."

"Do you want me to come with you?" Alessia asked.

"No, I'm okay," Milo said. "I could do with some fresh air."

"We just had a huge amount of fresh air," Alessia said. "In the Secret Garden."

"I think it's fine for Milo to just go by himself," Rosa said gently, and Milo gave her a grateful smile. "Alessia, perhaps you could show me some of these notebooks of yours. It sounds like you've collected quite the encyclopedia of information on your father; I am sure it's going to be invaluable."

Alessia was quickly distracted by the compliment, and Milo slipped out of the greenhouse, all the way back down the stairs to the wood and the lakeside where the Quip lay silently.

Milo put a hand on its side, and the cool feel of the Quip immediately calmed him. He liked Alessia a great deal and found the treehouse very beautiful and Rosa rather awe-inspiring. And yet he had spent so many years with only his uncle for company. Days would pass when he would barely even speak to Horatio, and years had passed without him talking to a single other person who wasn't inside of a book. And now there were so many people, and so many questions, and so many really, really important things to deal with. His head felt too busy and loud to even think. The noise, with all its expectations and decisions, was debilitating. He rested his hot forehead on the metal of the Quip and took some deep breaths in and out.

"One thing at a time," he said to himself. "That's all there is to it." He unlocked the Quip and climbed aboard to check the postbox set into the wall of the office. Anyone could send a letter to the Quip by addressing it correctly and tucking it into the Endpapers of a book; it was how Horatio had spoken to his book-smuggling clients and kept in contact with Rosa.

Milo opened the drawer under the postbox, and a few bits of post slid out. He quickly sorted through them, seeing several that were no doubt from Horatio's clients, unaware of what

had taken place over the last few days. He couldn't see anything on the creamy, thick stationery of the Alchemist, and he
double-checked there was nothing in his elegant handwriting.
However, there *was* a scrap of notepaper folded in half with his
and Alessia's name written hastily on the outside. He paused a
moment, debating whether he should wait for Alessia to open
it, but with a slight pang of guilt he sat down on the floor of the
Quip and read it by himself.

Dear Milo and Alessia,

*We just found your note. I'm sad that you went
without saying good-bye, but I know why you
felt you had to leave. I understand what it's like
when you know in your heart what you need to do
and people around you don't get it—I'm sorry if I
made you feel like that too. Horatio is safe with
us, and don't worry about Grandma and Grandad.
They were obviously worried when we realized you'd
gone, but they're happy to take care of Horatio
until you get back. They're mainly just concerned
about whether you're safe. I hope you remember
to check the postbox and see this, and I hope you
manage to find the Botanist and that she can help
you with the cure and deciding what to do about
the Alchemist. If you can, please tell us you got*

somewhere safely so Grandma and Grandad can
stop stressing out a little bit. And write if there
are any updates, or there's anything we can do to
help (or just write to me). Amelia is going to work
with my grandma to find out what they can about
the Alchemist via the Underlibrary. Grandma used to
work in the map room at the Underlibrary, so I'm
trying to remember as much as I can about the
Alchemist's Wizard of Oz map and what Alessia
said about it. Grandad says he might read some
murder mysteries in case they give him clues about
poisoning; I'm not sure how much that will help,
but he's still pretty weak from the poisoned book
and wants to help. Anyway, I hope you know how
to send letters back via the Quip or that you're
somewhere you can get in touch another way. I'll
write my mobile number on the back of this note,
and the Pages & Co. phone number and my email,
because I don't know if the Botanist has a phone
or a computer or anything—but just in case.

Love,

Tilly x

P.S. I haven't told my family about the whole
Anonymous Reader thing yet because I don't want
them to worry, but I did say that the Alchemist

wants this Book of Books. Remember to ask the Botanist about it! If you do find a way to get in touch, can you let me know if the Alchemist sends anything else to the Quip? I'm worried about what he might do when he realizes I haven't gone to the Botanist to do what he asked.

Milo refolded the note; it hadn't helped him feel much calmer. If he was honest with himself, he hadn't been thinking about Tilly at all when he'd left Pages & Co., and the threat to her and her family had been pushed to the back of his mind in his focus on finding out if his grandmother was alive—and finding the cure.

To abandon Tilly, especially given who Lina had turned out to be, sat uncomfortably with him. The Alchemist was so sure that Tilly was the fabled Anonymous Reader, the one book-wanderer who could find and open *The Book of Books* and discover all the secrets of bookwandering, that he'd concocted a terrible plan to get her to Venice. Archie Pages had only been poisoned so that the Alchemist would have leverage over Tilly. They should have a little bit of time before the Alchemist realized Tilly hadn't set out to get *The Book of Books* for him, but they needed to speed up this cure. They needed Horatio's answers, and they needed to find out where *The Book of Books* was being hidden before the Alchemist put Tilly in even more danger.

16

A Runcible Spoon

Even though he wanted nothing more than to stay on his own for a little longer on the Quip, Milo made himself get up and head back. He put his hand on the Quip once more, for a last boost of comfort and calm, and then started the walk back up the stairs to the greenhouse.

"Anything?" Alessia asked the second he opened the door.

Milo nodded. "Just a note for us from Tilly," he said, showing her the folded paper.

"How is Tilly?" Rosa asked. "All well at Pages & Co.?"

"Yes, so far," Milo replied. "They haven't heard from the Alchemist, and Horatio is being looked after. She did ask us to let her know that we got here safely. She left an email and a phone number if you have any way to use those?"

"I have both a laptop and a phone." Rosa laughed. "We are in a treehouse, not the Middle Ages. Would you like to call her?"

"I'll just text if that's okay," Milo said. "I want to keep going with the cure for now. If the Alchemist isn't putting Tilly and her family in danger at the moment, I think we should get that finished and hope Horatio can tell us more." It wasn't that this wasn't true, but there was also an unspoken reason: that he still felt guilty about leaving Horatio and running away without telling Tilly when she was potentially in so much danger.

"Of course," Rosa said, pulling a mobile phone, from her pocket. "Please feel free to use this, and perhaps it's good for Tilly to be able to get in touch if she needs to urgently."

Milo had never had a mobile phone, and he was embarrassed at how flummoxed he felt by the touch screen and seemingly endless options. Noticing his hesitation and without fuss, Alessia quickly took the phone out of his hand. Milo passed her the notepaper with Tilly's number and watched as she typed a message. She read it aloud as she did: "Hi Tilly, this is Alessia and Milo on Rosa's phone. Rosa is the Botanist, if you forgot. She lives in a treehouse—it's pretty cool. We are safe, and you can call us at this number if my father does anything dramatic or you need us. We found Milo's grandma, but she is also potentially ev—" She paused and looked sheepishly up at Milo. She deleted the last few words. "We found Milo's grandma and she is here too. We are working on the cure for Horatio and will call you when that is done. M & A." She looked back up at Milo, who nodded his agreement, and Alessia tapped send.

Alessia quickly added Tilly's number to the contacts list and passed the phone back to Rosa, who slipped it into her pocket.

"Shall we continue with the cure then?" she said. She brought over a piece of paper on which she had copied the ingredients list, and they all looked down at it.

1. Death made into life, to respect the work of the poison
2. A token of unnatural nature, to honor the power of the imagination
3. Something stolen honestly, to signify the gift of the cure
4. Something lost properly, for the time taken
5. An impossibility, to break the limbo they are held in
6. Ground ginger root, to soothe the patient on awakening
7. A seventh, for completeness: the record of the reader, for intent

"I think I might have an idea for ingredient number five—the impossibility," said Rosa, tapping that item on the list. "Books of course are full of impossibilities; much of what happens on the pages of a book is impossible outside of them. But this has to be a tangible thing that your father could distill and use himself. And I thought, well, where better to look for impossibilities than nonsense?"

"Huh?" Alessia said.

"Nonsense," Rosa repeated, pleased. "Nonsense poetry and suchlike—let's go down to the library and have a look under 'L.' 'L' for 'Lear, Edward.' Have either of you ever heard of a runcible spoon?"

"No," Milo said in confusion. "What is it?"

"Honestly, I don't know!" Rosa said. "Runcible isn't a real word, or rather it wasn't until Edward Lear made it up in a poem called 'The Owl and the Pussy-cat.'"

"Oh, I've heard of that!" Alessia said. "But I don't know it very well."

"It's a delightfully nonsensical poem," Rosa said. "Let's go get a copy of his poetry and I can read it for you—it's only short."

They headed from the greenhouse down to the library, where golden-hour sunshine was stealing through the windows, making the book spines glow. Rosa climbed up a ladder and pulled out a slim blue volume. After checking the contents list, she turned to a page, cleared her throat, and read aloud:

> *The Owl and the Pussy-cat went to sea*
> *In a beautiful pea-green boat,*
> *They took some honey, and plenty of money,*
> *Wrapped up in a five-pound note.*
> *The Owl looked up to the stars above,*
> *And sang to a small guitar,*
> *"O lovely Pussy! O Pussy, my love,*

What a beautiful Pussy you are,

You are,

You are!

What a beautiful Pussy you are!"

Pussy said to the Owl, "You elegant fowl!

How charmingly sweet you sing!

O let us be married! Too long we have tarried:

But what shall we do for a ring?"

They sailed away, for a year and a day,

To the land where the Bong-Tree grows

And there in a wood a Piggy-wig stood

With a ring at the end of his nose,

His nose,

His nose,

With a ring at the end of his nose.

"Dear Pig, are you willing to sell for one shilling

Your ring?" Said the Piggy, "I will."

So they took it away, and were married next day

By the Turkey who lives on the hill.

They dined on mince, and slices of quince,

Which they ate (here Rosa paused for dramatic effect) *with a*

runcible spoon;

And hand in hand, on the edge of the sand,

They danced by the light of the moon,

The moon,

The moon,

They danced by the light of the moon.

"Now isn't that wonderful?" Rosa finished with a satisfied smile.

"But what does it mean?" Milo asked.

"Well, it could be Lear's thoughts on all sorts of things," suggested Rosa. "Love, perhaps, or money, or his dining habits, or two outsiders running away. But also it doesn't have to mean anything in particular; it is nonsense poetry, after all. It can just *be* for the pure pleasure of reading it."

"But what's the difference between the good nonsense that we print in books, and the nothing-y nonsense that's silly and useless?" Alessia asked.

"Ever the scientist." Rosa smiled. "Well, did you like it? Did it make you feel anything?"

"Yes," Milo said, quite firmly, for he found that he really did like it. "But, when I think about it, I'm not quite sure why. I don't know how to describe it properly. It made me feel sort of . . . sort of like I'd just eaten something really tasty."

"I'd say that's an excellent way to describe it." Rosa smiled. "It is rather delicious, isn't it? You don't ever have to really know why you like a poem or a story or a book. If something in it speaks to something in *you*, then that's all there is to it. But for our purposes, I believe this poem might do nicely."

"A runcible spoon is an impossibility?" Alessia checked.

"I think so," Rosa said.

"I like it," Milo said. "Is there other nonsense poetry I can read?"

"Of course," said Rosa. "One of the most famous pieces of nonsense writing is something you likely will have heard of—the Jabberwocky poem by Lewis Carroll, who wrote *Alice in Wonderland.*"

"Can we get anything from there?" Milo asked. "Is there any"—he thought back over the various ingredients—"*unnatural nature* in that poem?"

"What a clever idea," said Rosa with an approving nod. "The Tumtum tree might be just what we need for the second ingredient. Another plant is definitely the best plan, as we certainly don't want to be trying to catch a Jubjub bird or a Bandersnatch and putting it over a fire to turn it into book magic."

"Are we supposed to understand anything you just said?" Alessia asked in confusion.

"It's all just nonsense." Rosa grinned. "Aren't you curious to see what it might look like? Let's start with 'The Owl and the Pussy-cat,' and work our way to 'Jabberwocky.'"

"Perfect," Milo said, and found that he was quite excited to see what bookwandering inside a poem might look like, especially one that was nonsense.

17

By the Light of the Moon

Given that they were reading themselves out to sea, Rosa found some waterproof jackets for them in the dressing-up box. They were too big for Milo and Alessia, so they rolled the sleeves up and added woolly hats. Rosa was wearing purple Wellington boots and a matching waterproof jacket.

"Milo, would you like to read us in?" she said, offering him the open book of poetry and linking arms with Alessia and him. Milo took the book and read out loud.

> *"The Owl and the Pussy-cat went to sea,*
> *In a beautiful pea-green boat."*

"Whoops!" Rosa said, but it was too late: the treehouse library started to click-clack down around them and then all of a sudden they landed heavily in a rather small, but undeniably beautiful, pea-green boat already occupied by an owl and a cat. It was nighttime and the stars reflected in the peaceful sea, which seemed to stretch on endlessly. For a moment the five of them stared at each other in surprise. It was a rather tight fit for five, not helped by the pots of honey, small guitar, and piles of cash in the bottom of the boat. Both the owl and the cat were almost the same size as Alessia and Milo, which was a little alarming. Milo found that he had rather expected them to be regular owl- and cat-sized, but then again, how would a normal-sized owl row a boat?

"Did I do it wrong?" Milo whispered to Rosa.

"Not at all," Rosa said. "It's my fault: this is the beginning of the poem, and they sail for a year and a day, remember?"

"Oh," Milo said, feeling a bit silly.

"No bother. Let's say hi and then just read ourselves to the right bit," Rosa said quietly and reassuringly. "It's rather fun to pop into this bit. Hello!" She turned to the owl and the cat. "We're dreadfully sorry for interrupting you, but your boat really *is* very beautiful."

"And congratulations," Alessia added, staring in awe at the large owl.

"Dear child," said the bird, with a tilt of its neck,

"Why do you offer us that?

We are set with supplies, do not think us unwise,

But we're merely an owl and a cat."

Milo was delighted to hear that the owl spoke in verse, just

like it did in the poem—even when it was confused about congratulations for a wedding that hadn't happened yet.

"Sorry," Alessia was saying. "I must've got you mixed up
with the other owl and pussy-cat I know. Who just got married."

"Worry not," said the cat.

"From where I am sat,

I can see where confusion may be.

If you know of a pair with a boat just as fair,

Who are also sailing the sea."

Milo could have listened to them speak endlessly, but Rosa
nudged him gently, and he focused on the book again. This time
he was careful to make sure they ended up *after* the pair had
sailed for a year and a day, and under his breath he tried again.

"So they took it away, and were married next day
By the Turkey who lives on the hill."

It was as if someone had pulled the plug on the sea
and everything was *rapidly sucked* in under the
boat as the night sky fuzzed and faded and
fell down to reveal a new scene.
It was still night, but Milo was relieved to find they were on
land again. The three of them were standing on a moonlit
beach, the calm, dark ocean stretching out in front of them.
The pea-green boat was tethered to a small pier that jutted into

the water, and behind them a gentle hill rolled away to a tiny cottage set on the edge of the sand, smoke curling upward from its chimney into the darkness and the window lit warmly from within. The door swung open, and the owl and the pussy-cat stepped out onto the sand, waving—or flapping, in the case of the owl—enthusiastically.

"Dear friends," called the owl, with a flap of its wing,

"Do share of the fare on our table.

We are dining on mince, and slices of quince,

Please eat as much as you're able!"

The three bookwanderers walked up the sand to the happy couple, who were indeed eating mince with quince. It did not look especially appetizing, but Milo politely took a slice of the fruit, which tasted a little like pear and was quite refreshing. Both the owl and the pussy-cat were eating with delicate golden spoons that resembled small ladles, with shallow scoops on one end and delicate loops of metal at the other.

"Those spoons are lovely," Alessia said. "I would love to try eating with one. Do you have any more?"

"'Tis a runcible spoon, to be used after noon,"

Said the pussy-cat, with great delight,

"Let me find you a spare, for to eat with more flair

Is much more pleasant at night."

The pussy-cat disappeared back inside the cottage, and they could hear

it rummaging around. Moments later it emerged holding aloft three more runcible spoons, which it happily gave to Alessia, Milo, and Rosa.

"This is very kind of you, thank you," Rosa said. Milo found he was rather disappointed they wouldn't be able to take the spoons with them just as they were. He would have very much liked to bring his runcible spoon home with him intact as a reminder of this lovely poem. As the owl and the pussy-cat kept eating their mince and quince, Rosa nudged the two children round the back of the house, where she slipped out the burner and bowl from her backpack.

"Let's get this done quickly," she said. "I don't want to distress the owl and the pussy-cat by burning their spoons." She lit the flame under the burner, added a drop of the rosemary oil to the bowl, and placed all three of the spoons there too. Milo was reticent to give his up, even though he knew there was no way for him to sneak it out. If Tilly had been there, he would have been tempted to ask her to hide one in her pocket so she could take it back to the treehouse and he could keep it. After a few moments, the delicately crafted spoons started to sparkle and crackle, their edges blurring and dissolving into pure book magic.

"And you're sure this rosemary method works?" Alessia said, staring at the fizzing spoons.

"Yes," Rosa said. "Of course, we're yet to be sure it will work in the cure, but I see no reason why not, based on my research. The rosemary just helps things along so the item remembers what it was—these spoons were made of imagination from the outset, and we're just doing this in order to get them back to the treehouse. Remember that the recipe calls for us to distill everything down anyway, so even if your father has worked out a way to get anything he liked out of books, he'd still be using this method, or one similar, to create his various concoctions. Right, I think we're done."

In the bowl, instead of three golden spoons, was a pool of rainbow, shimmering powder, which the Botanist carefully tipped into a glass bottle before tucking it safely away.

"Ready to go?" she said, and the others nodded, although Milo felt a strange yearning to sit by the sea and eat quince for a little longer.

"We should say thank you again," he said as Alessia turned to the page in the poetry book, ready to go.

"Of course," Rosa agreed, but when they headed back round to the front of the cottage, the owl and the pussy-cat had moved down to the edge of the sand, where they were waltzing gently, paw in wing, with the pussy-cat's head resting on the owl's feathery shoulder. And as Alessia read the last line of the poem, Milo watched in wonder as they danced by the light of the moon,

The moon,

They danced by the light of the moon.

18

Back in Time for Dinner

The walls of the treehouse library built themselves up around the bookwanderers.

"Well, that was a success, wasn't it?" Rosa said, smiling.

"We don't know if it's worked yet," Alessia pointed out.

"Fair, but we got what we went for without incident," said Rosa. "Let's stay positive for now, at least until there's reason not to. Right, while we're riding high on that success, shall we head straight to the Jabberwock? To get our 'token of unnatural nature'? Is everyone ready?"

"I don't suppose you have armor or anything similar?" Milo asked. "I really don't fancy meeting the Jabberwock."

"I'm afraid not," Rosa said. "But we'll be just fine. We can slip in, grab a Tumtum leaf, and be back out in time for dinner before we've even seen the Jabberwock."

Milo thought that was unlikely. He knew that time was of

the essence, that they needed to wake up Horatio as soon as possible, but he could feel his breathing speeding up again. After a lifetime of hiding in the background, it was overwhelming to be pushed into the spotlight so abruptly. Ever since they had picked up Tilly and Oskar on the Quip, it was as though someone had pressed the fast-forward button on his life and it was jammed on. Milo's mind was racing, and he could see Rosa's lips moving, but his brain wasn't taking in what she was saying until he felt Alessia's cool hand on his arm.

"Are you okay?" she said.

"Yes, I'm fine," he replied quickly.

"I don't think you are," Alessia said. "It's okay to say if you're not, you know."

Milo found it both reassuring and a little unsettling to have someone in his life who actually paid attention to how he was feeling.

"Rosa, is it okay if we just head down to the Quip quickly?" Alessia said. "We need to just check that . . . uh, the . . . that Milo remembered to lock the doors!"

"No one will stumble across it down by the lake," Rosa said.

"I just think we'd feel better if we double-checked before we bookwander away from the treehouse again," Alessia said.

"Of course," Rosa replied. "We'll go to Jabberwocky as soon as you're ready."

"We won't be long," Alessia said, and pulled Milo by the arm back down the wooden stairs to the grass.

"Thanks," he said as they walked toward the lake. "I don't know why I get so overwhelmed—it's embarrassing."

"Uh, maybe because this is all really overwhelming?" Alessia said. "Just an idea!"

"But no one else gets like this," Milo said. "You and Rosa were ready to go!"

"We all feel things differently," Alessia replied. "None of them are right or wrong. Just because I don't always show it, doesn't mean I'm not feeling it too. My tactic is to try and shove anything that makes me feel bad into a dark corner of my brain and hope I forget about it. I'm fairly sure that's not a recommended way of dealing with . . . well, anything, but it's how I got through living with my father. And look, I make jokes about bad stuff! And make people uncomfortable! Honestly, I think we're doing pretty well for two twelve-year-olds trying to stop someone from stealing the world's knowledge and imagination."

As they walked in the fresh air, and as Alessia spoke, Milo's breathing started to calm.

"Thanks," he said quietly. "It's pretty cool, you know, having a friend."

"It's not bad," Alessia said, grinning, but their laughter was cut short when they reached the gleaming Quip, as peering into the engine window was Lina.

"What are you doing here?" Milo said, and Lina spun round, looking undeniably guilty.

"Just having a nostalgic moment," she said, not making eye

contact with Milo, but keeping her hand on the Quip. "She is my train after all."

"No, she's not," Alessia said immediately. "She's Milo's. And before that she was Horatio's. She hasn't been yours for a long time now—because of how *you* used her!"

"I won't take any judgment from you, Miss della Porta," Lina said. "I do not particularly care to hear about your feelings on how I chose to run my own business. I see that you have not inherited your father's patience."

"That's not a word I'd use," Alessia huffed.

"He is a man who understands the importance of assessing a situation and putting a plan into motion that may take a lifetime to complete."

"It's easy for him, given that he has already lived many lifetimes," Alessia pointed out. "And he never seems to have shared that particular elixir with you."

At this, Lina fell silent and turned back to the Quip.

There was an awkward pause. Milo didn't want to unlock the Quip's door in front of his grandmother. He knew he wouldn't be able to refuse her inevitable request to come onboard, and Rosa's warning was ringing in his ears. They didn't actually need anything from the Quip, but they couldn't simply stand in silence looking at the train. It turned out that Lina didn't wait for Milo to open the door to make her request.

"Won't you give your old grandmother a last peek at her?" she said, turning and looking straight at Milo. "I would so love to just smell the spark of the engine again and see what Horatio has made of my office."

"I—I don't think . . ." Milo stumbled. Lina was fairly transparently not to be trusted, but she and Horatio were his only family, and Horatio was currently unconscious and in London.

"No," Alessia said shortly.

"It's not your decision to make," Lina snapped. "Milo is the Driver."

"Aha!" Alessia interrupted. "So you admit she's Milo's train!"

"Milo has the Driver's whistle," Lina said. "And the Quip answers to that. I don't debate it. But the Quip belongs to me, in her very soul. Don't you agree, Milo? I think you must feel it—a pull away from what you want. Of course, when you came here, perhaps it seemed like you were finally getting the hang of things. That's because she knew she was coming back to me, her true Driver."

Milo stumbled backward at her words, away from the train. Was she right? Was that the only reason he had felt so in sync with the Quip—because they were headed to Lina? He knew it was too good to be true: that he was the real Driver, that he and the Quip were operating so well together. But, at his upset, Lina's face changed.

"I'm sorry," she said, stepping away from the Quip toward Milo. "I don't want you to feel . . . I'm sure you're doing a very good job driving her for the moment, Milo. And . . ." She was stumbling over her words in a way Milo hadn't heard before.

"With all this excitement, I wouldn't want you to think that it's not very special for me to have found you again. I've never been very good at . . ." But she tailed off and glanced over her shoulder back at the Quip, which broke her attempt at whatever she was trying to get across. "Well, who knows what we could do as a team?" she finished. "Why don't we go onboard together?"

Silence hung among the trees like fog. Milo could feel Alessia resisting the urge to get involved, and he knew it had to be him who said no.

"I can't let you onboard," he whispered, and then turned and ran up the grassy slope to the treehouse, Alessia right behind him. When he emerged back in the library, flushed and anxious, Rosa stood abruptly.

"Are you okay?" she asked urgently. Milo shrugged helplessly; the question was too complicated.

"Lina was down by the Quip," Alessia answered. "Peering in the window and then asking Milo to let her in. She said she was the true Driver, which, I hope you know, is nonsense. She's just trying to wheedle her way back onboard so she has the power of the Quip in her hands. And goodness knows what she'd do with that."

"I don't know," Milo replied quietly. "I think she has a point about the Quip only arriving so smoothly because she's here."

"That's because you and the Quip are getting to know each other!" Alessia said. "Don't let her mess with your head."

"Alessia is right," said Rosa gently. "I am sorry that happened.

Lina can be like a ghost sometimes, slipping out of the tree-house, never being where I expect. As I said, I was worried she would try to access the Quip through you."

"Why do you even put up with her?" Alessia said angrily.

"Well, because I worry who else might take her in," Rosa said. "It's as simple as that. Bookwandering is safer with her here, and thankfully, while the Underlibrary is looking for her, she won't risk straying too far. Not to mention she has limited transport options, which is why it's important we don't let her on the Quip. You have the Driver's whistle with you, Milo?"

"Yes, always," he said, patting his chest where he could feel the whistle on its chain.

"Keep it safe." Rosa nodded. "Are you up for trying to get this next ingredient, do you think? I'll more than understand if you need a moment; it must be quite . . . unsettling to find your grandmother and for her to be . . . well, Lina."

"No, we should keep going," Milo said, steeling himself. "We need to keep going."

"If you're sure?" Rosa said, and Milo nodded firmly.

"Let's go find the Jabberwock," he said before pausing. "Well, hopefully not the actual Jabberwock, but you know what I mean."

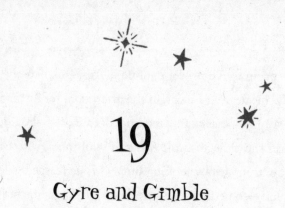

19

Gyre and Gimble

The Jabberwocky poem was in *Alice Through the Looking-Glass*, the sequel to *Alice's Adventures in Wonderland*. The stories of the two books always merged together in Milo's brain, but they were headed to where Tweedledum and Tweedledee lived as well as the Red Queen—and of course the terrifying Jabberwock monster itself. Rosa went to get a copy of the book.

"Now, Alice first reads the poem in a looking-glass book," Rosa said, studying the words in front of her. "She holds it up to the mirror and then she reads it out loud, and later she asks Humpty Dumpty about it. As we're after something from the poem itself, I think we should read ourselves in at the very beginning. Let's keep an eye out for slithy toves."

"What exactly is a slithy tove?" Milo asked nervously.

"I always forget which creature is which," Rosa said. "But there's a bit in the book where Humpty Dumpty explains a lot of the poem to Alice—let me find it. Yes, look here, he says that 'brillig' means four o'clock in the afternoon, for instance."

"Yep," Alessia said, reading over Rosa's shoulder. "Four o'clock, the time to broil things for dinner. And a borogove is . . . a 'thin shabby-looking bird with its feathers sticking out all round—something like a live mop,' and a mome rath is 'a sort of green pig' that's 'lost its way.' We could definitely use one of those for a bit of unnatural nature, I reckon!"

"I'm not killing a borogove or a mome rath!" Milo said firmly.

"You wouldn't really be killing it," Alessia said practically. "You'd be distilling it back into imagination, which is where it came from."

"I'm not sure that would make much difference for me, or for it," Milo said firmly.

"Personally, I'm totally fine killing a mome rath," Alessia said with a shrug. "I have some rage to get out of my system. So any mome rath that even looks at me funny better watch their step."

"No one needs to kill anything," Rosa said firmly. "Mome raths or borogoves."

"What do you think you'd even bag a borogove with?" Alessia pondered.

"Okay, okay, can we please focus?" Rosa said with a clap.

"I'm just saying that if I happen to catch a slithy tove while we're getting the Tumtum leaves, will anyone have a problem?" Alessia asked with a determination in her eyes that Milo found a little alarming.

"Let's just see how we get on," Rosa said. "A slithy tove is not worth dying for."

"You haven't seen one yet," Alessia said. "I have a feeling they're going to be *magnificent*."

Rosa exchanged an amused glance with Milo. "Shall we then?" she said, and the three of them linked arms again, and this time Rosa read them in.

> "'Twas brillig, and the slithy toves
> Did gyre and gimble in the wabe:
> All mimsy were the borogoves,
> And the mome raths outgrabe."

The cozy treehouse library slid down on all sides to be replaced by an altogether less appealing sight. A dense and damp forest surrounded them, and a sharp breeze made Milo shiver with cold. The smell of rotting fruit hung in the air, and when combined with the wet and mulchy leaves underfoot, the whole place felt as though it were decomposing into putridity around them. The trees grew unpleasantly close together, their branches wrapping around each other as though trying to suffocate their neighbors, and their trunks dripped with a slimy sort of dampness. A slate-gray sky was only just visible between the tightly grown leaves that towered above them.

A chattering, rustling sound was impossible to ignore

behind them, and they turned to find the strangest creatures Milo had ever seen dancing around a—

"Is that a sundial?" Milo said in surprise.

"Of course," Alessia said, taking the book from Rosa and flicking further into it. "Look, here. Humpty Dumpty explains it—the slithy toves 'make their nests under sundials' and they 'live on cheese.' Rosa, I should've asked you for some cheese as bait. I can't believe I didn't think of it. And here, the wabe is the grass plot around a sundial. So, these are the slithy toves! Gyring and gimbling!" Alessia looked absolutely delighted as she edged slightly closer to the sundial and watched the toves, who looked like small badgers—but their black-and-white bodies were scaly not furry, and they had a sort of twisty tail and snout, like a corkscrew.

"Go easy on your ankle, Alessia," Rosa reminded her, but Alessia was entranced by the strange little beasts.

"They're very odd," Milo said, unsure he liked looking at them as they ran round in circles, some of them digging little holes in the squelchy ground.

Suddenly Alessia darted forward and grabbed one.

It wriggled and wriggled in her arms, but she held firm, and before too long it fell quiet and snuggled into her chest, to Alessia's immense pleasure. "I wish Tilly were here so I could take him home as a pet," she said, stroking its strange scaly head. "They're so cute!"

Milo did not agree, but it was certainly much cuter than whatever had just emerged from the trees. Something that looked like a cross between a brown flamingo and a mop had emerged onto the path in front of them, and it was perhaps the most pathetic thing Milo had ever seen. It stared at them with doleful eyes, feathers sticking out in every direction, before crossing the path and disappearing back into the trees on the other side.

"A mimsy borogove," Alessia said sagely, as though they were on safari. "Only the mome raths to spot now. I think that strange whistling noise must be them." But before they could lay eyes on a mome rath, a man burst down the path in front of them. He barreled right into Milo and put his hands on his shoulders.

"Beware the Jabberwock, my son!

The jaws that bite, the claws that catch!" he shouted into Milo's face.

"Oh no, you've made a mistake," Milo said, backing away. "I'm not your son, and don't worry, I already . . . *beware* the Jabberwock. I don't want to meet him at all."

"Beware the Jubjub bird, and shun

The frumious Bandersnatch!" the man continued, ignoring Milo.

"I swear, I don't want anything to do with any of them!" Milo said. "Please, you're looking for someone else."

The man didn't acknowledge what Milo had said, but instead produced from a scabbard a shining sword, pressing it into Milo's hand.

"'Tis here, for you, the vorpal sword.

Take care, my son, and rest a while.

Look there, the Tumtum tree abides

To lean upon before your trial."

Milo tried not to take the sword, but the man closed his hands around the pommel so that Milo had to take it or drop it in the mud.

"This really isn't mine," Milo protested in horror. "I don't know what to do with a sword, I don't want to have a trial, and I don't want to fight the Jabberwock."

"Sir, I think you've confused Milo with someone else," Rosa said, putting a reassuring hand on Milo's shoulder. But the man would say nothing else; he only scampered off down the path, leaving the three of them staring in confusion at his back, Milo still holding the vorpal sword.

"Well, at least we can use it to chop something off the Tumtum tree," Rosa said. "And now we know which one it is because that man pointed it out. Why don't you two go and cut a bit off while I get my kit ready?"

But before Rosa could even take her backpack off her shoulders, they heard an almighty roar from very, very close by, and then through the trees burst the Jabberwock, eyes aflame.

20

Snicker-Snack

"**G**ive it here!" Alessia shouted, gesturing for the sword, which Milo was still clutching, frozen at the sight of the Jabberwock. The monster was the most terrifying thing Milo had ever seen, a horrible mix of a dragon crossed with a giant snake. Its face, lolling from the end of a long, scaly neck, looked like something from the very depths of the ocean, with bulbous, angry eyes, spindly long antennae, and horrible spiky fins sticking out from its jowls. Leathery wings flapped raggedly above its head as its taloned claws scraped along the trees.

The Jabberwock let out a horrifying, bloodcurdling screech as it approached, cutting Alessia and Milo off from where Rosa was standing with her backpack.

"Milo!" Alessia yelled again.

"We need to GO!" Rosa hollered, but Alessia wasn't passing the book or flicking to the last page. Even if she had, there was no way to get to Rosa so they could be touching and leave together. Alessia had abandoned the book on the ground and was trying to yank the sword from Milo's grip. And all the while, the Jabberwock lumbered closer.

Milo unfroze and let go of the sword, eagerly letting Alessia take it, but she immediately dropped it.

"How can you lift it?" she shouted, trying to pick it up once more and failing.

Milo was terrified and confused—the sword wasn't particularly heavy, and yet Alessia could barely pry it from the mud. And the Jabberwock crashed ever closer, hissing as it came. Its eyes, Milo realized, were fixed on Alessia, who was entirely focused on, and frustrated by, her inability to lift the sword. If someone didn't do something, the Jabberwock was going to lunge at her. *Why isn't someone doing something?* was the only thought chasing itself around Milo's brain, and then, all at once, time seemed to slow and crystallize.

He was still terrified, but a clarity settled on his senses.

All the injustice and anxiety and guilt he was holding seemed to channel down his arms and tingle in his fingertips.

He thought of Horatio and the Pages family and Alessia and fixed his eyes on the Jabberwock's horrible face and, without breaking eye contact, bent down and picked up the vorpal sword.

He grasped it firmly, and even though he had never held a sword until a few moments ago, he found that its weight felt solid and comfortable in his hand, and he instinctively knew just how to hold and to swing it.

He darted forward, and just before the Jabberwock lunged at Alessia, who was now staring up at its dripping jaws in terror, Milo struck.

Snicker-snack!

And the Jabberwock fell. The second it was done, that charge of clarity entirely abandoned Milo, and he thought he was either going to be sick or burst into tears. He sat down abruptly on the wet ground, shell-shocked.

"That was AMAZING!" Alessia said, throwing herself down on the dirt and flinging her arms round him. "How did you do that?!"

"I don't know," he said truthfully.

"How could you even lift the sword?" Alessia said, a little enviously. "You're not any stronger than me."

"Definitely not," Milo said, smiling for the first time. "Maybe it's because that man gave it to me, so I touched it first? I've no idea."

"It was clearly meant for you," Rosa said, joining them on the ground, rather pale-faced. "You were very brave, Milo."

The three of them sat silent for a moment, breathing heavily, staring at the very unappealing remains of the Jabberwock, but the moment of calm was interrupted by another rustle of bushes. Milo reached urgently for the sword before they realized it was just the man from before, returning to see the slain monster.

"And hast thou slain the Jabberwock?

Come to my arms, my beamish boy!

O frabjous day! Callooh! Callay!"

He chortled in his joy. He yanked Milo to his feet and wrapped his arms round him.

"Ah yes," Milo said awkwardly, extricating himself from the embrace. "Callooh, callay, quite."

"O frabjous day!" the man repeated, planting a kiss on Milo's forehead before scampering back into the forest, hopping jauntily over the Jabberwock's body.

"I always forget what it's like coming to someplace Lewis Carroll wrote," Rosa sighed. "Never a dull moment. Shall we finish this and get back to safety?"

Milo nodded, still rather stupefied. Alessia turned back to the Tumtum tree and plucked a few leaves, peeling off a strip of bark as well. She handed them carefully to Rosa, who was efficiently setting up her burner and bowl.

While they waited for the bark and leaves to disintegrate into pure imagination, Alessia managed to pick up another tove from under the sundial and tried to convince Milo to pet it.

"It'll make you feel better!" she said, holding the strange corkscrew animal—which hissed disapprovingly at Milo—out to him.

"Uh, no thank you," he said warily. "I'm fine."

"Suit yourself," Alessia said, stroking the animal's scaly head and whispering sweet nothings to it. "When we next see

Tilly," she promised it, "I'm going to bring her here and we'll find you and take you home and you can come and live with me."

"I take it you're not up for turning it into book magic for the antidote after all?" Milo said, smiling again wearily.

"How dare you," Alessia said, looking offended that he'd even mentioned it. She tried to put her hands over the creature's ears, before realizing that it didn't seem to have any. "Don't listen to nasty Milo," she murmured to it in a baby voice. "I never said such a thing."

As Rosa finished decanting what had been the Tumtum leaves and bark into a bottle, Milo laughed and lay back on the damp ground. If Horatio could see him now . . .

21

Hero of the Hour

The three of them arrived back in the treehouse muddy and exhausted but satisfied.

"Goodness," Rosa said, taking off her backpack. "Well, that was unexpected."

"I'm not sure how unexpected the Jabberwock appearing in a poem about the Jabberwock was," Milo said, trying not to say it in an "I told you so" sort of voice.

"Fair enough." Rosa smiled. "It just all happened a bit more quickly than I was expecting—I thought we'd have more time. I hadn't quite anticipated that man arriving and presenting you with the vorpal sword, Milo. I've been to that poem before, and he's never turned up so speedily. I'm not sure what was different. But the key thing is that we're back safely. And we have four of the seven ingredients for the cure."

"Death made into life, a token of unnatural nature, an impossibility, and ginger," Alessia listed.

"More than half." Milo nodded, pleased.

"Now I think it's time for a shower and then dinner, don't you?" Rosa said. "And we can plan where we might be able to get hold of something *stolen honestly*. I could also do with a quick word with Lina."

Alessia let Milo use the shower first, due to the Jabberwock blood, and Milo willingly accepted the offer. He wanted to wash the mud and the smell of that forest and its monsters off his skin as soon as possible. The wooden bathroom cabin felt like a tiny sauna, with perfectly hot water falling from the showerhead and filling the room with steam. There was a bottle of lavender-smelling soap, which he used generously, and a pile of soft white towels waiting. He was shaking a little bit, post–monster slaying, but he also sensed something he hadn't before—a sort of warmth in his stomach, and a touch of the clarity that had settled on him still remained. Perhaps this was what confidence felt like, he thought. He found that he quite liked it.

Changing into fresh clothes also felt very good, and he headed back down to the kitchen to let Alessia know the shower was free. Alessia and Rosa were chattering away about alchemy as Rosa stirred a pot on the stove and Alessia, sitting at the table, chopped up salad. Nutmeg the squirrel was perched on the windowsill, nibbling an acorn.

"There he is," Rosa said when she saw Milo. "Hero of the hour. Slayer of the Jabberwock!"

Milo blushed.

"I just had to stop it from, you know, eating Alessia," he said.

"I'm very appreciative." Alessia grinned, passing the salad knife to Milo so he could take over. "I'd definitely prefer not to be eaten by a Jabberwock. It's not a very glamorous way to go."

Milo started chopping tomatoes as Alessia headed for the shower.

"How are you doing, Milo?" Rosa asked as she stirred what Milo could see was a pot of risotto.

"Okay," he said automatically.

"Is there anything you'd like to ask me?" she offered.

"Do you think the ingredients will work? To wake up my uncle?"

"I think they have a good shot, yes. Between the three of us, we know a fair amount about the Alchemist and how his brain works, so I think we can be pretty confident we're interpreting the recipe accurately enough."

"And will we take it to Pages & Co. once it's done?"

"Yes, although we might have to go there before it's even ready," Rosa pointed out, "if we need Tilly's help to get to the Lost Property Office at the Underlibrary."

"Oh yes," Milo remembered. "Tilly is safe, right?"

"I won't lie to you—Tilly isn't safe as long as the Alchemist thinks she is the only way he can get hold of *The Book of Books*," Rosa said. "But I don't think she is in any immediate danger. I'm hoping that tomorrow we can check on the Pages family on the way to the Underlibrary, and she'll be safe until then."

"Do you know if she really *is* this Anonymous Reader the Alchemist thinks she is?" Milo asked.

"No," Rosa said. "We won't know for definite until the powers of the Anonymous Reader are put to the test. That is, until someone tries to actually access and read *The Book of Books*."

"You can't even read it?"

"Nope," Rosa said. "It would be too much power for one person. You can't have the same person protecting it and being able to read it—it would be a lot of temptation for anyone to bear."

"It does seem likely that it's Tilly, doesn't it? As she has so many special abilities."

"I agree we should seriously consider that it might be Tilly, yes. But it wouldn't be for her special abilities, as you put it; it would be because of her relationship with stories. The Anonymous Reader symbolizes *all* readers and storytellers, not just bookwanderers. Now, I think this risotto is ready. Do you want to set the table? I'm sure Alessia will emerge any moment."

Five minutes later Rosa was serving up butternut-squash risotto for Milo and Alessia when the kitchen door opened and there stood Lina.

"Eating without me?" she said with a wry smile.

"I was going to bring you a bowl up later, Lina," Rosa said steadily. "As I mentioned when I popped up earlier."

"Don't worry," Lina said. "You don't need to walk on tiptoe around me. Everyone can calm down. I'm not going to go sneaking through my only grandson's belongings and steal the Driver's whistle. Who do you take me for?"

Her words had the opposite effect she intended, and Milo suddenly felt even more strongly that there was a distinct possibility she might do just that. He resisted the urge to check that the whistle still hung safely round his neck, not wanting to alert her to where it was.

Rosa dished up a bowl of risotto for Lina, and there was an awkward pause as they started to eat.

"How are you getting on curing my son then?" Lina said.

"We've found some of what we need," Rosa said. "In large part down to the bravery and ingenuity of these two. We were about to discuss where we might find the next ingredient on the list."

"Oh, come now, you can speak freely in front of me," Lina said with a cough. "There's not much I can get up to these days. A glance at the Quip is hardly so scandalous. My son and I may not be on the best of terms, but I would prefer him alive and awake—at least do me the credit of believing that. And I could do with something to get my brain going. Let me help. Please." Her voice cracked a little at her final words, and Milo wanted to believe that her concern for Horatio was sincerely meant. Rosa glanced at Milo, who nodded his agreement.

"We need to find something that has been stolen honestly,"

he explained. "It has to come from a book because it needs to be made of imagination."

"Interesting," Lina murmured. "Of course, Geronimo made his recipes poetic. He always used to tell me he had—"

"An artist's soul," Alessia finished with a roll of her eyes.

"Quite," Lina said. "'Stolen honestly,' you say?"

"'To signify the gift of the cure,' that's what's written," Milo added.

"So, something that has been taken, but for good reason, perhaps?" Lina mused. "There's one thing that immediately springs to mind for me. I can think of someone who steals from the rich and gives to the poor . . ."

"Robin Hood!" Milo said in excitement. "Of course!"

"It's a strong suggestion," Rosa agreed. "A clever idea. And, as long as we avoid the Sheriff of Nottingham, it shouldn't be too dangerous to acquire. Alessia, do you think that fits? I'm not sure your father strikes me as a big fan of the redistribution of wealth."

"You mean given that he's literally trying to gather all the world's knowledge and keep it for himself?"

"Precisely," said Rosa.

"I think he probably sees himself as some kind of Robin Hood, if I'm being honest," Alessia said. "He genuinely believes he's acting for the benefit of bookwanderers and the whole world, that too many of the people in charge at the moment make terrible decisions, and that he'd be much better at it."

"He's not wrong about the first part," Rosa said. "But I don't believe there's any one person who should be in charge of that much of *anything*."

"I agree, but my point is that I think my father probably quite admires Robin Hood, for breaking all the rules and following his own instead, even if the two of them seem to have very different outlooks to us. We should look at a copy of the book and see what it says."

"A good plan," Rosa said. "We'll head to the library after dinner."

"Robin and I actually go way back," Lina chimed in.

"It's no surprise to me at all that you and Robin Hood have a history," Rosa said.

"I will come with you then," Lina continued. "I'll be able to help talk to him and get what you need."

"No," said Rosa abruptly.

"I don't mind a bit of danger," Lina said.

"You know this isn't about danger to *you*," Rosa said. "Although romping through a wood *would* be dangerous for you. You are not supposed to be bookwandering."

"Let's not forget it's my son we're trying to save," Lina said coldly.

"Who is poisoned because of the man you worked with and so clearly still admire!" Rosa said angrily.

"You cannot control me," said Lina stonily.

"But I can," said Rosa. "Your choices led you here: your

decision to work alongside a man you knew was immoral, and your prioritization of your own schemes over the well-being and safety of others, including your own family. You are fortunate to have ended up in this place, at the behest of your son, and not in disgrace and alone as you would have been without him. You will stay here at the treehouse, and you will not be coming with us."

At that, Lina put her coffee mug down and without saying anything left the warm kitchen. Milo and Alessia sat in slightly uncomfortable silence.

"I'm sorry about that," Rosa said, her cheeks still a little flushed. "It must be upsetting for you to see, Milo. I am sorry

your grandmother is not . . . well, not what you might have perhaps hoped for. She is a complicated woman who does not enjoy other people's rules. But all will be well; please don't worry."

"Okay," Milo said quietly, not sure what else there was to say. He felt embarrassed and awkward and had to quell the desire to apologize for the chaos his family had caused—and was still causing.

"I hope you're not feeling responsible for your relations," Rosa said gently. "You're your own person, Milo. We're shaped by the people around us, yes, but they do not make us completely. We can *always* choose who we are, and we can always choose to change. That applies to both of you," she added, reaching over the table and taking Alessia's and Milo's hands, one in each of hers. "You get to decide who you are and what you stand for, always remember that."

22

Stolen Honestly

After dinner the three of them went to find some Robin Hood stories in the library.

"There are lots of different versions," Rosa said. "I'd be lying if I said I could tell you off the top of my head who wrote them all."

"So how will we find them?" Milo asked.

"The catalog of course," Rosa replied. "You can't have a library without a catalog." She opened the laptop on one of the desks and typed "Robin Hood" into the search bar, laughing at Milo's and Alessia's reactions to the up-to-date technology.

"How do you even get Wi-Fi here?" Alessia asked.

"Alessia, you must stop being surprised that we have things like phones and internet here!" Rosa laughed. "It's just the countryside!"

"Yes, but we *are* up a tree," Alessia retorted.

"But one with all—well, *some*—mod cons," Rosa said.

"Anyway, here we go! I have an edition of Robin Hood stories by someone called Howard Pyle, so let's look under 'P.'"

The book was easy to find, and Rosa started skimming through it.

"How about this for a plan," she said. "I take this to bed with me and read it properly so we can find the best bit of the story to bookwander to. I'll also have a look at your uncle's coded notebooks. And after we all get a good night's sleep we'll be ready for a trip to Sherwood Forest and the British Underlibrary tomorrow. There's no way we could have done much more today anyhow."

While one part of Milo was keen to press on and find as many of the ingredients as possible today, most of him was yearning for a soft bed and sleep, so he agreed happily.

"But listen," Rosa added. "This bodes well." And she read aloud a section she'd found:

> *"So, in all that year, fivescore or more good stout yeomen gathered about Robin Hood, and chose him to be their leader and chief. Then they vowed that even as they themselves had been despoiled they would despoil their oppressors, whether baron, abbot, knight, or squire, and that from each they would take that which had been wrung from the poor by unjust taxes, or land rents, or in wrongful fines. But to the poor folk they would give a helping hand in need and trouble and would return to them that which had been unjustly taken from them."*

"Perfect." Alessia nodded. "What could fit the 'something stolen honestly' clue better? This one's going to be easy."

Rosa marked the page with a slip of paper. "Let's not get ahead of ourselves. I'll find a story where they actually do steal, and we can head there tomorrow morning. And we need to have a proper look at those Records too, but we're on the home stretch, I think. Excellent work today—now let me show you where you're sleeping."

They followed Rosa up to the third level, where a bridge connected the main platform to a cozy cabin perched in the treetops, fairy lights strung around its door. Inside was a twin bedroom with a narrow but comfortable-looking bed on each side of the space. The wooden beds had high sides, which meant Milo felt like he was lying inside a snug little ship when he climbed in. The sheets were white and soft, and the room smelled of wood, cotton, and fresh air.

"Have you got everything you need?" Rosa asked from the door. "I expect you'll wake with the sun, but I'll bring you some cups of tea or juice if I haven't heard from you by nine, okay?"

"Thank you," Milo said.

"Good night, Milo," Rosa said as she pulled the door closed. "Good night, Alessia. I'm glad you're here. Sleep well, for after all we are such stuff as dreams are made on."

Smiling at the thought of Will Shakespeare, the author of those words and his and Tilly's companion on their quest to save the British Underlibrary, Milo closed his eyes. He had intended to keep talking to Alessia about everything that had happened, but a gentle snore drifted over from the other bed, and he realized Alessia was asleep already. It wasn't long at all before Milo joined her, and they both slept soundly as the tree branches rustled against the walls and the moonlight slipped in through the window.

23

Countdown

Milo woke up to the late summer sun filtering through the pine branches and into the cabin. He felt, for the first time in a while, well rested.

"Did you sleep okay?" he called to Alessia. There was no response. He assumed she was still sleeping, though when he sat up and stretched he saw that she wasn't in bed at all. His instinctive reaction was a heart-lurching panic, but he stopped and told himself firmly that she had probably just woken up earlier and was eating something delicious in the kitchen—which was exactly where he wanted to be. Getting changed quickly, he headed down the stairs where he did indeed find Alessia, eating a thick slice of toast covered in honey.

"Good morning, Milo!" Rosa said. "I was just about to come and wake you."

"I'm sorry I slept in," he said.

"Oh, don't apologize!" Rosa said. "You didn't sleep in! It's not even nine o'clock—we won't see Lina for hours yet. Alessia was up not long after me; she's an early bird."

Alessia gave a grin as she crunched her toast. "I'm used to getting up early and sneaking around from living with my father," she said. "And old habits die hard."

"Can I get you some breakfast?" Rosa asked Milo.

"Thank you," he replied. "Whatever you have."

"We have toast, as you can see and hear, or eggs, or cereal, and plenty of fruit," Rosa listed.

"Just what's easiest!" Milo said cheerfully, not wanting to cause a fuss.

"Well, I was just about to make myself some scrambled eggs," Rosa said. "If you'd like that too?"

"That sounds great, thank you," Milo said. "Is there anything I can help with?"

"You're fine," Rosa said. "You sit down. Cup of tea? Orange juice?"

"Orange juice, please," Milo said, and settled down next to Alessia. "Have you been up long? What were you doing?"

"Rosa was showing me the Robin Hood stories in the library," she replied. "We left the book up there before breakfast, ready for us to bookwander."

"What did you make of Robin Hood?" asked Milo.

"Not quite what I expected," Alessia said, "not in this version, at least. I suppose there are lots of different Robin Hoods in lots of different books. But I think there are some promising options for a part of the story where they've stolen something for the good of others."

"I also had a look at those Records," Rosa said. "I'm not sure they're going to be any use for the cure; the pages are almost entirely blank now. But the Alchemist doesn't strike me as someone who would create something so clever and intricate and then have it all hinge on something like this. In fact, I think that's perhaps the genius of the cure—that there are multiple ways the recipe can be interpreted, so it's harder to make, *but*, if you do understand what the clues to the ingredients mean, it has failsafes built in should one ingredient become unavailable. Having said that, I'm not quite sure what we could use to replicate a reader's Record, as it's part of their own imagination. Maybe a bit of the person themselves?"

"Ew," Alessia said under her breath.

"Just an idea," Rosa said. "Don't worry, *you* don't have to drink it."

"Did you manage to check my uncle's notebooks?" Milo asked.

"I did, but I'm afraid I haven't had much luck yet," Rosa said. "I'm sure you noticed that he seems to use initials when referring to people, but the rest of it doesn't fit with any codes I know off the top of my head. I think our best bet at this point is to try and wake him as soon as possible and leave decoding the notebooks as a last resort."

Rosa was putting Milo's plate of scrambled eggs on the table when her pocket started vibrating. Pulling out her phone, she glanced at the screen and passed it to Milo.

It read: *Matilda Pages.*

"Hello?" he said as he answered.

"Milo? Is that you?" Tilly's voice came down the line. Alessia was gesticulating at him, and he shrugged his confusion, so she sighed and grabbed the phone from his hand, pressing a button and putting it on speakerphone.

"Hi, Tilly, it's Alessia," she said. "And Milo and Rosa are here too. We can all hear you."

"Are you okay?" Milo asked urgently.

"Uh, sort of," was the reply. "We are, at the moment, but we just had a package delivered. And it's from the Alchemist."

Rosa dropped her mug on the floor, where it spilled hot coffee over the wooden boards.

"Are . . . are *you* okay?" Tilly's voice came.

"Yes, sorry, Tilly," Rosa said. "And hello, it's lovely to be speaking with you. I hope we'll have the chance to meet in person very shortly. What did the Alchemist send you?"

"It's a clock," Tilly said.

"Huh?" Milo asked, but Alessia looked more nervous.

"Some kind of countdown?" Alessia said.

"How did you know?" said Tilly.

"It's very much his style," Alessia replied. "I'm sure it's very beautiful."

"Yes," Tilly admitted. "It's not got a proper face—you can see all the workings, all the cogs going round."

"That's all well and good," Rosa said, letting the coffee seep into the floor, "but what is it counting down *to*? Did he send a letter?"

"Yes," Tilly said. "Let me read it to you."

Dear Matilda,

I trust you and your family are well. I sent you a letter via the Sesquipedalian discussing our future plans and working relationship. In it I said that in exchange for the safety of your family, and that of Milo Bolt, you would bring me The Book of Books. I had hoped you were on your way to the Botanist to acquire this for me, but I have been informed by my contacts that you remain in London at Pages & Co. and that your grandfather is awake thanks to the stolen dose of the cure I presume Artemis assisted you in completing. I can only assume you did not see my first missive, and so I extend you the courtesy of repeating my offer here to ensure there is no doubt between us. I have enclosed a clock which will stop at exactly six o'clock, British Standard Time. I am a reasonable man and therefore do not expect you to have retrieved The Book of Books by then, but I do expect you to have confirmed that you will seek it out, by choice, so that I do not have to resort to less elegant, and more pressing, forms of negotiation. You can contact me via the Endpapers of any edition of The Wizard of Oz and it will reach me here in Venice. If you prefer more modern methods, I leave my telephone number below. If you give Tommaso your name, he will ensure you reach me with haste.

I look forward to hearing from you shortly, as I am sure you understand the severity of the situation and that there is no limit to what I will do to acquire The Book of Books.

Yours,

Geronimo della Porta

There was a brief moment of silence as the three at the tree-house took it in.

"So you have until six o'clock today to tell him if you will find the Book?" Milo summarized.

"Basically," Tilly said. "And I hadn't actually got round to telling my grandparents or mum about the fact that he thinks I'm the only one who can get *The Book of Books* till just now. I didn't want them to worry, but, needless to say, they are *quite* worried. Is the Book there with you?"

"No," Rosa said. "I know where it is, but it isn't here. Okay, what we're going to do is this. Tilly, I think we're going to need Horatio to finally defeat the Alchemist, and we have to get an ingredient from the Underlibrary to complete the cure. So, we are going to come to Pages & Co. now to collect you, and then we'll go to the Underlibrary to get that ingredient, hopefully with Ms. Whisper's help. After that we'll come back to the shop to pick up your family and bring them here."

"Can the Alchemist get to you there?"

"I don't know," Rosa said. "It would be naive to think he hasn't worked out where I am, despite the veil of book magic trying to keep this place secret. But, once we're here, we can work out another plan if need be, or even hide in a book temporarily. But we need to get your family and Horatio away from Pages & Co. before the deadline. Does that make sense?"

"But what about the other ingredients?" Milo said.

"We can go to *Robin Hood* afterward," Rosa said. "Someone can go there quickly and get whatever we need, and then we'll only have the Record ingredient to work out. We'll have everyone safe here along with what we need to make the cure and wake up Horatio. Once we've done that and learned what he knows, we can work out our next stage. Yes?"

"Yes," chorused the three children.

"Hang tight, Tilly," Rosa said. "Tell your grandparents to start closing up the shop and getting together what they need, and to have Horatio ready to move. We'll be with you very soon."

"Did you notice that my father assumed Artemis helped us complete the cure?" Alessia said quietly.

"What?" Milo asked, not having focused on that bit in the letter.

"It didn't even cross his mind that I'm the one who has his recipes, that I know anything useful at all."

Rosa put a calm hand on Alessia's shoulder. "I rather think that his underestimation of you will be a key part of his downfall," she said.

24

A Fair Sight Was Nottingham Town

"Are we okay leaving Lina here?" Milo asked.

"Yes, I think so," Rosa said. "I do venture out now and again, and for all her protestations she knows she's safest here—she's upset or betrayed too many bookwanderers to have many other options. But perhaps you could take her a cup of green tea and let her know we're going to the Underlibrary and that we'll be back soon. It's probably best to prepare her for the Pages family arriving—and Horatio."

Milo put the kettle on, choosing a cheerful yellow mug. Once the tea was made, he set off carefully up the stairs, trying not to spill the hot drink on his fingers. Lina's door was closed and he knocked gently, but there was no answer.

"Lina?" he called. "It's Milo, I've got a cup of tea for you! Are you up? We're going to go to the Underlibrary in a minute." There was still nothing, so he pushed the door open a crack and peered through. Sunlight spilled in, and he saw that the room was completely empty. The bed was neatly made and the windows were cracked open, letting in a fresh breeze.

"Lina?" Milo called again, venturing slightly farther, calling for his grandmother even though he knew she wasn't there. There was only the one room, and it was quite clearly empty. "She must have gone down to the library," he tried to convince himself. But as he stepped backward, eyes on the tea mug, his foot caught on something on the ground. It was a book, lying open on the floorboards. Milo crouched down slowly and picked it up, meaning to simply put it somewhere out of the way, but as he glanced down and went to close it, he saw that the text inside was moving on the page.

"A fair sight was Nottingham Town on the day of the shooting match. All along upon the green meadow beneath the town wall stretched a row of benches, one above the other, which were for knight and lady, squire and **dame, and rich** *burghers and their wives; for none but those of rank and quality were to sit there. At the end of the range, near the TARGET, WAS A RAISED SEAT BEDECKED WITH ribbons and scarfs*

*and garlands of flowers, for the Sheriff of
Nottingham and his dame. The range was two-
score paces* **broad. At one end stood the target,
at the other a tent of striped** *canvas, from the pole
of which fluttered many-colored flags and stream-
ers. In this booth were casks of ale, free to be broached
by any of the archers who might wish to quench their
thirst, and any passing folk who wished to glimpse
the competitors and beg a glass of ale,*
as one elderly *woman did."*

Milo would never have realized there was anything amiss
if the words had not been changing in front of his eyes. He had
never read any version of the Robin Hood stories himself, but
that was irrelevant as the sentences were undeniably moving—a
sure sign that a bookwanderer was inside. Abandoning the mug
of tea, Milo pelted down the stairs to where Rosa and Alessia
were waiting in the library. He thrust the book at them.

"I think Lina's gone to get the next ingredient herself," he
gasped, out of breath.

"What?" Rosa said in confusion.

"Look," Milo said. "There's a bookwanderer in here. I
found this in Lina's room. She was angry that you said she
couldn't come with us, and I think she's just gone without telling you."

"Blast," Rosa said, grabbing the book and studying the shifting words. "She must've come and got it from the library while we were eating."

"But why is the book still here?" Alessia pointed out. "She's supposed to take it with her, otherwise how will she get back?"

"And you're sure she's not in her room?" Rosa checked with Milo.

"Definitely not," he said. "This was on the floor, open at this page. Would she have dropped it? I thought she knew what she was doing with bookwandering?"

"She does, or rather she used to, but she doesn't bookwander any more than I can help it," Rosa said. "She isn't so well these days, so perhaps the feeling of bookwandering after a long gap shocked her and she dropped it. But, as the book is here, I don't see how it could be anyone else in there. And we need to get to Pages & Co."

"Not until six," Alessia said.

"I don't think we want to cut it that fine," said Rosa.

"No, of course not," Alessia said steadily. "But it is only just past nine o'clock in the morning, that's nine whole hours before my father's deadline. We can go and get Lina, and the last ingredient while we're there, and then go on to Pages & Co. and the Underlibrary after that. Then Lina will be safe, we'll have the ingredients, and we can pick up the Pages family all before six. You said yourself that you think we're going to need what Horatio knows to defeat my father for good."

"You're right," said Rosa, going over the numbers. "There's no reason this should take very long, and we can set off straightaway after. I don't think we can leave Lina in there with no way to get out, and who knows what she's getting up to? We can only hope that it's just the ingredient she's trying to find. We have time."

"Let's go then," Milo said, linking arms with the other two and reading them into the book.

"Across the range from where the seats for the better folk were raised was a railing to keep the poorer people from crowding in front of the target."

25

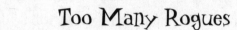

Too Many Rogues

At once the treehouse started to dissolve around them and was replaced with a noisy, bustling meadow on a crisp and frosty autumn day. Milo checked the title of the chapter and realized Lina had come to an archery competition where Robin Hood was competing incognito.

Milo, Alessia, and Rosa were standing right outside Nottingham, the town's wall running along one edge of the field. Benches were laid out for the rich people, who were sitting in their silks and furs and velvets. More and more well-to-do people kept arriving in small carts or on horses bedecked with bells on their reins. On the other side of the meadow were the poorer observers, who were standing or sitting on the grass, kept behind a railing to keep them from straying onto the shooting green. At one end of that green was the target, and opposite was a great colored tent hung with flags—where the ale casks were kept, and where Milo had seen Lina in the text.

The line had read them onto the poorer side, where there was an atmosphere of rowdy celebration, with people claiming good spots to observe the shooting, and families playing and laughing as they waited for the competition to start.

"Mark my word," Milo overheard a man saying to his young son, "'tis a day for fine shooting—there will be the very best archers come to this match. Look, there's Gill o' the Red Cap, the Sheriff's own head archer."

"And that there's Adam o' the Dell," another man said, pointing to an archer in the tent. "A man of Tamworth, of three-score years and more, who in his time had shot in the famous match at Woodstock."

Milo, Alessia, and Rosa picked their way through the crowds.

"This would be pretty good fun if it weren't for the clock ticking," Alessia said, swiping a pie from a passing tradesman without him noticing and tucking in. Milo found that he agreed, and decided he'd come back once everything was fixed. Before they could reach the tent, the crowd stilled as one, a great hush falling in the air as everyone looked up. Milo trained his eyes to the same spot to see a grand man riding on a white horse with a beautiful woman on a brown horse next to him. The man was wearing a purple velvet cap that matched his fur-trimmed robes. Underneath his robe, his clothes were a deep blue-green color, his shoes were pointed and black, a great golden chain hung round his neck, and a huge red gem fastened his collar. He was

quite a sight. The woman was dressed no less grandly, although a little less ostentatiously, in a blue velvet dress trimmed with white feathers. They were quite clearly the most important people there. Milo checked the book.

"It's the Sheriff of Nottingham," he whispered to Alessia.

"I figured." Alessia nodded.

After the pause that had met their arrival, the crowd erupted into shouts and cheers. When the Sheriff and his wife were settled on the fanciest seats, the ones covered in flags and flowers, a man stood and blew three clear notes on his silver horn, and the competing archers stepped forward in a line, prompting more cheers and whoops from the crowd as they spotted their favorites, like it was a medieval football match. Milo started to move toward the tent, but at the call of the herald everyone quietened again, and it was impossible to pick their way forward without drawing attention.

"The rules of the game are as follows," the herald proclaimed loudly, his voice singing out into the air, clear as a bell. "Shoot each man from yon mark, which is sevenscore yards and ten from the target. One arrow shooteth each man first, and from all the archers shall the ten that shooteth the fairest shafts be chosen for to shoot again. Two arrows shooteth each man of these ten, then shall the three that shoot the fairest shafts be chosen for to shoot again. Three arrows shooteth each man of those three, and to him that shooteth the fairest shafts shall the prize be given."

"Huh?" Alessia said.

"I think he said that all of them shoot, and the best ten get to go again," Milo said, reading the text in the book to check. "And then the best three from that go again, and then the best of *them* is the winner."

"And why has Lina come here?" Alessia asked.

"I suppose for the prize," Milo said, trying to work out what it was. "One of the archers is Robin in disguise so he can win the prize from under the Sheriff's nose. Oh yes, look, the prize is a golden arrow. Presumably he's going to win that and sell it to raise money to help people."

"So, it's the arrow we need," Rosa said. "I hope that's what Lina is after too."

As the archers lined up and the crowd jostled for a good view, the three bookwanderers managed to make their way to the far end, right by the colorful tent. With the archers out on the green ready to compete, it was deserted except for the casks of ale—Lina was nowhere to be seen.

"Can you see where she is in the text?" Rosa asked Milo, who was flicking through the few pages beyond the point where they'd read themselves in, to see where the words were moving.

"I can't see anything changing," he said. "Maybe she's gone off page."

"Not a surprise," Rosa muttered in frustration, losing her cool for once. "She's perhaps looking for a way to get out. Goodness knows what she would have done if you hadn't noticed the text moving, Milo. It's just typical of her approach to do something so selfish and—" She stopped. "I'm sorry, Milo."

"It's fine," Milo said. He'd only spent a day with both Lina and Rosa, and even though he wished it were otherwise, he already knew better than to trust his grandmother over the Botanist. Having found the ale tent empty, they slipped behind the benches where the rich people sat, hoping to find Lina somewhere tucked away from the action.

"Is he here, good sir?" Milo heard the Sheriff's wife ask her husband quietly as they passed behind the couple.

"There is no one clad in Lincoln green," the Sheriff replied. "Nevertheless, he may still be there, and I miss him among the crowd of other men. But let me see when ten men shoot, for I wot he will be among the ten, or I know him not."

"I don't know the Robin Hood stories very well," Milo whispered to Rosa. "The Sheriff is the baddie, right?"

"Oh yes," Rosa said. "Very much so, and Robin Hood's sworn enemy. But Robin always has one over on him, as he will prove again today."

"So, Robin is one of the archers?"

"He is," Rosa said. "Although I'm not sure which one from here; they do all look quite similar, don't they, apart from the colors they're wearing."

She was right, as they were all men between the ages of about twenty and forty, almost all with beards and long hair.

One at a time they stepped forward and took their shot, and Milo couldn't help but be impressed as the arrows whistled through the air, many of them cleanly finding the target at the other end of the range. The best ten were selected, and the rest were dismissed into the crowd. Six of the men were courting the crowd, their names being chanted in delight. Milo tried to pick out their names, enjoying the strange sounds of them. He heard calls for Hubert o' Cloud and Diccon Cruikshank among the cacophony of shouts.

"But which one is Robin?" Alessia asked Rosa as they stayed hidden behind the benches, trying to spot Lina in the crowd, knowing she must be staying close to the competition if she was after the arrow.

"Have a look in the text, Milo," Rosa was saying. "Can you tell? I can't remember the details, but he wears something that marks him out, so he must be the one with the patch over his eye, or is he the tall one in blue?"

"Now seest thou Robin Hood among those ten?" the Sheriff was whispering to his manservant.

"Nay, that do I not, your worship," the man replied nervously. "Six of them I know right well. Of those Yorkshire yeomen, one is too tall and the other too short for that bold knave. Robin's beard is as yellow as gold, while yon tattered beggar in scarlet hath a beard of brown, besides being blind of one eye. As for the stranger in blue, Robin's shoulders, I ween, are three inches broader than his."

The Sheriff gave a disgruntled huff, smacking his leg in annoyance.

"Then yon knave is a coward as well as a rogue," he said. "And dares not show his face among good men and true."

"To my mind," Rosa muttered under her breath, "that's at least one too many rogues for one day."

26

A Principle, More Than a Practice

The ten men who had progressed to the next round all shot again, twice, and the three best of those remained on the green to rapturous cheers. They were the man with the eye patch, and the men they called Gill o' the Red Cap and Adam o' the Dell of Tamworth Town. They could hear plenty of calls for Gill and for Adam, but none for the other.

"I guess we have our answer," Alessia said, pointing to the scruffy-looking man in the eye patch.

Milo nodded. He kept trying to read ahead to work it out for sure, but the writing was old-fashioned and dense, and he kept getting distracted by the fact that the story was really playing out in front of him with lords and ladies in velvet and feathers, amazing archers and disguised heroes. There was no hope of moving around without detection now that it was down to the final three, for the crowd was quiet and focused, disrupted only by the odd cry of a baby or call for one of the competitors. Gill stepped up first.

"Lina won't be able to do anything until the arrow is won," Rosa said. "It has to be stolen first, remember? It still belongs to the Sheriff. I don't want to risk bookwandering forward and not getting the right spot, so, as much as we can, let's just try and enjoy the show. It won't take long now."

Gill pulled out an arrow with a broad feather and drew his bow carefully; the arrow flew through the air and hit the target just shy of the center.

"Now, by my faith," the Sheriff cheered. "That is a shrewd shot!"

The man with the eye patch came up to shoot next, provoking unpleasant titters of laughter from both sides of the crowd. He looked very unkempt, his clothes dirty and stained, and clearly the crowd doubted his aim despite having witnessed him get this far. He drew the bow and shot quickly, within moments of stepping up to the mark, and his arrow somehow managed to sit even closer to the center than Gill's. The two arrows were so near each other on the target than their feathers were nestled together.

Finally, Adam stood and shot, his arrow joining the gathering at the center. Milo couldn't see whose was best. The men shot again, and it became clear that while all three were very talented archers, the man Milo knew to be Robin was just that crucial fraction better. They had one more to go, and Gill once more shot a beautiful, straight arrow, a whisker away from the center, and was once again just bested by Robin's, which hit the very heart of the target. Adam took one look and shook his head.

"I shoot no more this day," he said, unstringing his bow. "For no man can match with yon stranger, whosoe'er he may be." He bowed to Robin and left the field.

And so, the competition was won, and the crowd, suddenly on this stranger's side, erupted into cheers. The Sheriff gave a sigh and hauled himself to his feet, approaching the man.

"Here, good fellow," he said. "Take thou the prize, and well and fairly hast thou won it, I bow. What may be thy name and whence comest thou?"

"Men do call me Jock o' Teviotdale, and thence am I come," said Robin-in-disguise.

"Then, by Our Lady, Jock, thou art the fairest archer that e'er mine eyes beheld, and if thou wilt join my service I will clothe thee with a better coat than that thou hast upon thy back; thou shalt eat and drink of the best, and at every Christmastide fourscore marks shall be thy wage. I trow thou drawest better bow than that same coward knave Robin Hood, that dared not show his face here this day. Say, good fellow, wilt thou join my service?"

"Nay, that will I not," Robin replied, and Milo could hear the anger in his voice. "I will be mine own, and no man in all merry England shall be my master."

"Then get thee gone," cried the Sheriff, and his voice

trembled with rage. "And by my faith and troth, I have a good part of a mind to have thee beaten for thine insolence!" Then he turned upon his heel and strode away.

"Quick, we need to follow Robin," Milo said, reading ahead. The three of them slipped out from behind the benches, among the well-to-do who were leaving speedily after the Sheriff's displeasure had been made clear, wanting to stay in his good graces. The poor were leaving too, although Milo was sure he could hear some repeated calls of Robin's vow to remain his own man. The three of them hurried after Robin, who strode into the edges of Sherwood Forest.

"We should've just read to this bit," Alessia moaned. "He's going too fast. My ankle is starting to hurt again." But she was too loud, as at her complaint Robin whirled round.

"Who goest there?" he called. "I warn thee, coward, do not vex me."

"We aren't going to . . . vex you," Milo said awkwardly.

"And we're not cowards," Alessia said, affronted. "We just need that arrow."

"Nay, my sneaking friends," Robin said, smiling as he saw his pursuers. "For it is merely two children and a maid."

"What's that supposed to mean?" Alessia said. "You don't think we could fight you?"

"Goodness, Alessia," Rosa said as Robin roared with laughter. "Sir, we are not here to fight, but we do ask if we could have your arrow."

"For what dost thou need it?" Robin said. "I have won it by my own wits and wiles, and I wish to surprise my friends. They shall cheer and laugh and write poems and songs about how wise and generous I am!"

"Aren't you going to give it to the poor?" Milo asked, a little unsettled by Robin's demeanor. "Or sell it and give the takings to people who need it?"

"What jests!" Robin said. "Perhaps, but then again perhaps not! Once I have given my merry men—and Marian—a good tale, I thought I would use it to taunt the Sheriff. I shall find no satisfaction if he knowest not that it was I who tricked him thus."

"But isn't helping the poor your whole thing?" Milo asked, confused.

"Why yes," Robin said, puffing his chest out. "But, child, these are matters for those of us who have made our way in the world for more years than thee. Think of it as a principle, more than a practice. The spirit we labor under. And do not misunderstand me, we help those who need it, but we help ourselves too, what jests!"

"So, you're more about the stealing from the rich bit," Alessia said, hands on her hips. "And less about the giving to the poor side of things."

"Who are thou to judge me, child?" Robin said with a pout. "Will ye not come to meet my merry men—they will be most jovial when they hear of how I, Robin Hood of Sherwood

Forest, once more triumphed over yon Sheriff. I thought to tie a scroll to the arrow and shoot it through the Sheriff's window. I would write . . . I would write . . . Well, I must think upon it, something witty shall come to mind, I am sure."

"We have great need of that arrow," Rosa said. "It will help save the life of someone dear to us."

Robin paused. "It will help to save a life?"

Milo nodded.

"Why didst thou not tell me this before?" Robin said. "I shall be sure to aid thee. But first I must relate my tale to my friends, and then I must shoot the arrow at the Sheriff, and then I shall trick it from him another time, and then you may have it, my dear friends." And he smiled at them as though he were doing them a great favor.

Milo looked at Rosa in despair: they couldn't exactly wrestle the arrow out of Robin's hands even though Alessia looked primed for a tussle.

"Let's leave him be for now," Rosa said. She dipped a curtsy at Robin, who gave her a wink and bounded away into the forest.

"You let him go!" Alessia said in disappointment. "I could've got it, I swear!"

"We can worry about him later," Rosa said. "Remember, we're working against the clock, literally. We can come back for the arrow, but right now we need to find Lina. I assumed she would be going after the arrow too, but we haven't seen her. I would really prefer not to leave her here while we go to

Pages & Co. Any sign of her on the page, Milo?"

Milo opened the book to the end of the chapter they were in, where Robin went to meet his friends and dramatically revealed himself as the archery victor before they feasted and laughed. Distinctly, Robin did not seem to use the arrow to help anyone except himself.

"I did think when I was scanning through the book that it was lighter on the giving to the poor than I thought," Alessia said. "Rosa noticed too—before we were in such a rush, we were thinking of trying a story where he takes some money from some beggars because he thinks they have too much, although that sounds a bit dodgy to me. Maybe he gets nicer in more modern versions and does more donating. We should see if there's a more recent edition at Pages & Co. Although I swear I could've got that arrow if you'd given me more time." She stared after Robin a little wistfully.

"I've got her!" Milo shouted as he noticed a squiggle on the page. In the paragraph where Robin boasts of his triumph, the words were moving and shifting with mention of a woman praising Robin, but then, all of a sudden, she disappeared again.

"She's gone," he said. "She's gone off page."

"Not so far off page that I can't find my way back," a voice said from behind them, and the three of them turned to see Lina limping through the trees, a golden arrow in her hand.

27

Style Over Substance

"What on earth were you thinking?" Rosa said in frustration, rushing toward her.

"I was expecting a little more thanks given I've found your ingredient," Lina said, breathing heavily with exhaustion.

"Why exactly did you go by yourself? And how were you planning on getting back?" Rosa said, taking Lina's arm to support her and ignoring Lina's comment.

"I didn't *mean* to drop the book," Lina said, clearly slightly embarrassed at having done so. "But once I was here there wasn't much to be done about it except hope that you'd notice—and look, you did. And otherwise, well, I suppose I would've joined Robin's band of merry men, swapped one treehouse for another. I've dealt with worse."

Milo didn't say anything, as he was having an unpleasant realization.

"When did you take the arrow?" he asked Lina.

"Just now of course," she replied.

"But we spoke to Robin, and he isn't going to use it to raise money for people who need it, he's just using it to score points against the Sheriff. I—I don't think it counts as something stolen honestly; it's just regular stolen! And we're running out of time to find something that does count."

"There's plenty of time," Lina said defensively. "It's not my fault you misread the story, Rosa."

"I'm not going to lower myself to argue that point," Rosa said carefully. "And we don't have plenty of time. Geronimo has sent Tilly a countdown clock and an ultimatum—which you might have known if you'd been in your room for Milo to tell you, rather than off gallivanting here."

Milo was struggling to manage his disappointment—in his grandmother for her recklessness, in Robin Hood for not being much of a hero, and that the arrow wouldn't work for the cure.

"There must be some story we can use," he said. "Why would Robin Hood have this reputation otherwise? Alessia, you read that bit out where they said they were going to help people."

"I guess it's style over substance," Alessia said. "Lots of people promise lots of things they don't deliver on."

"And people like to look good," Rosa added. "They often have lofty ideals that they struggle to hold fast to in the end."

"It's just . . . It's just not good enough!" Milo burst out in frustration. "We need to have another go!"

"Another go at what?" Alessia asked in confusion.

"At making Robin Hood do the right thing," Milo answered. "We have time still."

"I'm not sure we *do* have time," Rosa said. "And even if we did we would need to take Lina back first. Perhaps Alessia can stay with her."

"No way," Alessia said. "I'm doing whatever Milo is doing."

"And I—" Lina started, but was cut off by Rosa.

"You have caused enough trouble already," Rosa said. "Let's go back to the treehouse and decide our next move from there. I don't think it's wise to all stay here."

"Fine," Milo said, and read the last line of the book to take them back to the treehouse.

"And now, dear friend, we also must part, for our merry journeyings have ended, and here, at the grave of Robin Hood, we turn, each going his own way."

28

Start at the Beginning

As the now familiar wooden walls of the treehouse reassembled around them, the final words about the grave of Robin Hood sank in. Milo turned to Alessia, Rosa, and Lina.

"I'm sorry, Robin Hood *dies* at the end of the book?" he said, thinking of the larger-than-life man they'd just met. "How sad."

"Sounds like it," Alessia said as matter-of-factly as ever. "He is just a man after all; he has no magical powers or anything."

"The thing about books," Lina added quietly, "is that no one in them ever really dies, because you can always start again at the beginning. Robin Hood will never truly die so long as he's in these stories. If only real life worked the same."

Milo looked at his grandmother in surprise. She wiped her eyes abruptly, not wanting them to see her emotions.

"Hang on," he said. "You're right. We're forgetting really simple bookwandering stuff here. You've just reminded me—*you can always start at the beginning*! We can try again and get it right this time." He looked Rosa in the eye.

"I'm going back into the book, to get this arrow or work out something else," he said. "There must be something. We have to finish the cure, and we still have time. We can just choose a different moment—we were too early last time. We need to speak to him when Robin gets back to his men in the wood."

"It's not safe," Rosa said. "You're in my care here; I don't want you to go without me where I can't help. And you know time inside books is unpredictable."

"I am very, very grateful for everything you've done for us," Milo said, trying to keep his voice firm. "But it's my uncle we're trying to save, and Alessia's father that we're trying to stop. Look, hardly any time has passed since we went in—only a few minutes!"

"He's right," Lina said. "I went too early. He'll have a good shot later on, I think."

"Did you just admit you got something wrong?" Rosa asked, taken aback.

"Not wrong," Lina said with a grin. "I could have finessed it though, perhaps. You should let Milo try if he wants to. Underneath I think he's as stubborn as his grandmother."

Rosa nodded her acceptance.

"I won't stop you, Milo," she said. "It's your decision. Please be safe and be quick. I will get everything ready to go for when you return. Here, you'll need this." She passed him her backpack with her imagination kit in it. Milo had been expecting more resistance to his plan and found himself flummoxed by an adult trusting him to make his own decisions.

"Okay," he said in the end as he put the backpack on carefully. "Well, thank you. Alessia, are you coming?"

"Obviously," she said, linking arms with him. And this time Milo read them right to the tree where Robin was about to make his triumphant reveal.

"It was a right motley company that gathered about the noble greenwood tree in Sherwood's depths that same day. A score and more of barefoot friars were there, and some that looked like tinkers, and some that seemed to be sturdy beggars and rustic hinds; and seated upon a mossy couch was one all clad in tattered scarlet, with a patch over one eye; and in his hand he held the golden arrow that was the prize of the great shooting match."

29

A Little More Revolutionary

Milo and Alessia emerged among a ragtag group of people, which meant that, despite their modern clothes, no one paid much attention to them. All eyes were on the man in red who had won the shooting match, the man Milo and Alessia knew was Robin Hood. He clapped his hands together, stood up, and then slowly, for maximum attention and drama, took the patch off his eye and pulled away the red rags he was wearing to reveal a finely cut outfit of green.

"Easy come these things away," he said with a cheeky grin. "But walnut stain cometh not so speedily from yellow hair."

"That is very clever," Alessia said to Milo. "I will admit that."

"Rubbing a few walnuts on your hair doesn't make you a hero," Milo said, still decidedly unimpressed by Robin Hood.

"I didn't say it did!" Alessia hissed. "I just said I admire his ingenuity."

"Well, I don't," said Milo. "I'm pretty over adults disappointing me at the moment. I'm not in the market for another one."

Alessia laughed. "I like this new Milo," she said.

"What do you mean?"

"You know, standing up for yourself, doing what you think is right, not being won over by Robin," Alessia said. "I like it."

"You mean Robin and his fancy walnut beard and green outfit?" Milo said, giving Alessia a teasing elbow in the ribs.

"Hey!" she yelped, grinning. "He may be a little ridiculous, but I'd be lying if I said I wasn't going to rub a walnut on my hair later on and see what happens."

Their stifled giggles were lost in the general uproar of noise as the group cheered Robin's deception of the Sheriff. As Robin paraded around, showing off his bow and the arrow, people started to set up a great feast in the woods to celebrate. Long tables emerged, together with stools made of sawn-off tree trunks. Heaps of food appeared from some tucked-away kitchen to go with the rather large pig that had been roasting on a spit in the clearing. There were bowls of vegetables: potatoes and carrots and turnips all roasted with what smelled like rosemary. Great big loaves of bread were sliced roughly and generously. There were large, steaming pies topped with golden pastry, whole grilled fish, and a great vat of a rich, dark stew. Everything smelled incredible, and if they'd had time to spare, Milo could have sat down and eaten a huge portion, even though he had just had breakfast.

"I think we should eat," Alessia said, staring at the food as if hypnotized.

"We don't have time," Milo said. "And we just ate."

"I'm not turning down some of that pie," Alessia said. "And I think we'd be better off going about this subtly—we need to convince Robin that it's the right thing to do. I don't think he's a bad sort really; he seems to at least believe in the principles of charity, even if he's not very good at actually doing it. We've got to be clever about this—watch."

Alessia stood up and went over to the table, cutting herself a hearty portion of pie before sitting next to a stout man wearing rough brown robes tied with a rope round his middle and a cross round his neck. Milo went to sit behind them so he could hear, taking a plate of roast vegetables and stew as he went. No point letting this woodland feast go to waste, he thought.

"Hello, Father," Alessia said to the man. "Friar Tuck, am I correct?"

"Why yes," he said merrily. "But I do not know thee, and you do not look to be from these parts."

"I'm a friend of Robin's," Alessia said smoothly. "I spied him at the archery competition and knew it was him from the way he shot."

"A clever lass then," Friar Tuck said. "For he fooled all else. I would that I could have seen him deceive the Sheriff so roundly, but I am sure Robin will find a way to illuminate the Sheriff as to his foolishness."

"I heard he had some silly plan with the arrow," Alessia said as she ate, managing to sound very casual and relaxed. "I for one was a little disappointed, I must admit."

"Whyever would thou sayest such a thing?" Tuck said, looking shocked.

"I just thought our enterprise was about giving to the poor," Alessia said. "You know: steal from the rich, give to the poor."

"It makes for a pretty saying, that is true," Tuck said. "And our band doth swear to support those in need. But not so many opportunities have yet arisen; we are still coming together and . . . discovering our purpose. We will of course turn our eyes to charitable pursuits, I am sure. And we have aided those who needed assistance—Robin has given much already."

"He has?" Alessia asked.

"Aye, Robin says that when we discover injustice we must divide the wealth into three: let the rich keep one-third, donate a third to the poor, and we take the other," Tuck said. "To feed and clothe ourselves."

"So, the wealth is not really *stolen*, is it?" Alessia asked. "If the rich get to keep some of it."

"A curious question," Tuck replied. "But nay, not stolen. Robin is most persuasive but remains most respectful of the church and nobility and would not leave them in poverty. He merely encourages them to help those more in need."

"I think you could be a little more revolutionary, to be honest," Alessia said matter-of-factly. "The principles of the redistribution of wealth are solid, but to my mind could be taken further to have a real impact."

"I suppose there is always more that can be done," Tuck said, clearly somewhat unsettled by Alessia's manner.

"All I'm saying," she went on, mouth full of pie, "is, do you not think it would be a grand and gracious gesture to give the arrow to those in need? The Sheriff would be sure to hear of his gift being donated, and it would bring him endless rage to know that it was Robin Hood who had won, and done this with the prize."

"Thou art a generous lass," Tuck said, "and what you say is kind and wise, but it is Robin who will decide what is to be done."

"But I have heard you are kind and wise too," Alessia said. "And persuasive. 'The moral core of the group,' that's what I heard people saying around camp, and that Robin listens to you above everybody else, that he prizes your judgment the most. I am sure he would always want to know what you think of such things."

Tuck blushed pink with pleasure.

"Well, look, Robin is standing," he said. "Let us hear what he wishes."

30

A Very Strong First Draft

R obin was indeed standing and clearing his throat to gain everyone's attention.

"My friends," he called. "What feasting we have had! What jests! But truly I am vexed in my very soul, for I heard the Sheriff say today, 'Thou shootest better than that coward knave Robin Hood, that dared not show his face here this day.' I would fain let him know who it was who won the golden arrow from out his hand, and also that I am no coward such as he taketh me to be!"

Another man stood and spoke. "Good master," he said. "Take I, Little John, and Will Stutely, and we will send yon Sheriff news of all this by a messenger such as he doth not expect!"

"Pray tell me more of this jape," Robin said, clapping his hands in delight.

"We shall write on a scroll to taunt him and tie it to the

very arrow you stole," Little John said. "And shoot it through his very window while he sups!"

"Oh, what jests!" Robin said. "Wait, wait, I am composing it at this very moment!" He climbed onto his stool, flung an arm out, and said:

> *"Now heaven bless thy grace this day*
> *Say all in sweet Sherwood*
> *For thou didst give the prize away*
> *To merry Robin Hood!"*

He paused, awaiting applause that eventually came, led by Little John.

"Bit awkward, don't you think?" Alessia whispered to Tuck.

"Aye, I have heard better rhymes," Tuck admitted.

"Bit embarrassing for everyone if you send that through the Sheriff's window, perhaps?" she went on.

"Nay, child," Tuck resisted. "'Tis all merriment and will bring Robin great pleasure to ensure the Sheriff knoweth he is no coward."

"But think what that arrow could do for those in need," Alessia pushed. "On the one hand, you can shoot an arrow with a bad poem through this guy's window; on the other hand, you could live up to your reputation and principles. You're clearly a man of faith." She put a hand on Tuck's arm and looked earnestly into his eyes. "I think I know what God would rather you do."

At that, Tuck stood and waved to attract Robin's attention.

"Robin," he said. "Bravest and truest of us all, I have set to thinking and perhaps this is an opportunity to walk a higher road and"—he turned to Alessia to jog his memory—"to live up to our reputation and principles," he went on. "What would be a greater ignominy to the Sheriff than realizing that not only had the brave Robin Hood stolen his prize right from under his very nose, but had proceeded to aid the impoverished people the Sheriff himself has left to suffer?"

"Well, go on, what dost thou propose?" Robin said impatiently.

"That we sell the golden arrow and give the proceeds to the poor."

There was a slight pause that turned to general murmuring, and then all heads turned to look at Robin to see his judgment.

"Hmm," he said. "A noble thought, Tuck, and thou knowest I love to help, 'tis what all say of me, but it seems that it is of *great* import the Sheriff knows I am no coward."

"I am sure you can invent a ruse of even greater amusement to ensure that he doth!" Tuck said. "And mayhaps, as we go about our plan, we can write another verse. Yours was a very strong first draft, but I believe you have even greater words of wit within you."

"I hearest your sayings," Robin said, fidgeting. "And I see that many here are eager to know my pronouncement."

Milo thought he looked decidedly shifty, as though he regretted this conversation was taking place with everyone listening.

"Steal from the rich! Give to the poor!" called a voice that sounded distinctly like Alessia.

"Hear, hear!" Milo shouted, and then, soon enough, everyone there was chanting it to Robin, who had no choice but to make it seem as though it was what he wanted all along.

"Aye! Steal from the rich and give to the poor!" Robin called. "'Tis what I have long said! Tuck, thou must take this arrow right away and ensure it is used to help those in need. I will speak to Little John about how we can make certain the Sheriff knoweth what has occurred this day. Quick, take it now!"

Tuck hurried forward and took the arrow and found Alessia and Milo already by his side.

"Excellent work, Father," Alessia said, clapping him on the back enthusiastically, alarming him. "A rousing speech and a convincing argument! Now, why don't you have a tankard of ale to celebrate a point well made? Allow us to put the arrow somewhere safe while you enjoy your feasting."

Friar Tuck could clearly not keep up with Alessia and was entirely flummoxed by this child who had appeared and so confidently talked to him, and now here he was, holding

Robin's arrow. He gave it to Alessia in a daze, and she bobbed a curtsy.

"What an honor to meet you, Father," she said, and yanked Milo away before the friar realized quite what had happened.

"That was amazing," Milo said in awe as they stumbled through the trees away from the feast.

"It did go rather well, didn't it?" she said, pink-cheeked with happiness. "Now I hope we can get Rosa's kit to work properly—we need to get this arrow distilled and back to the treehouse as quickly as we can. And I need some more of her ointment; my ankle is throbbing."

Once they had found a quiet spot, tucked away among the trees, Milo unpacked Rosa's bag, taking the burner and bowl out carefully and setting them down on the grass. He lit the flame easily with the matches in the kit and selected a sprig of rosemary from a vial, placing it gently in the bowl alongside the arrow, which was far too long to fit and was just balanced on the top.

"It's going to take too much time like that," Alessia fretted.

Milo picked the arrow up desperately and laid it across a rock on the ground before stamping hard on the feathered end. To his relief it snapped easily at the thinnest spot, and he could place the gold feathers in the bowl with the rosemary. Before long the rosemary started to release its aromatic scent, and the arrow began to spark and glitter.

"Here we go," he said, urging it onward.

"Thank goodness it's working," Alessia said, hopping from one foot to the other as she watched the trees for any sight of Robin or Friar Tuck.

"It's going; it's going," Milo said, getting an empty bottle ready as all of a sudden the arrow finally dissolved in a flurry of pure book magic. Milo poured the mixture into the bottle as quickly as he dared, stoppering it firmly. He tossed the burned rosemary into the trees, stashed the kit away, and gave Alessia a thumbs-up.

Just then a voice came from the direction of the clearing. "You there! Have you seen two children holding an arrow? Did they come this way?" Milo and Alessia looked at each other in alarm as Friar Tuck burst through the undergrowth, cursing in a most impious sort of way.

"Now!" said Milo.

Alessia had the last page ready to go and, grabbing Milo's arm, she read them back again to the treehouse.

"And now, dear friend, we also must part, for our merry journeyings have ended . . ."

31

Outside the Realm of Possibility

As the treehouse materialized around them, Milo and Alessia let out a simultaneous breath of relief.

"We did it!" said Milo. "Well, it was mostly you, really. Hang on, where are Rosa and Lina? We can't have been gone long at all."

"I guess Rosa's in the greenhouse getting ready?" Alessia said.

"I'm kind of glad we'll have missed whatever conversation they had about Lina going into *Robin Hood* without telling anyone," Milo admitted.

"Would've been interesting to listen to though." Alessia shrugged. "We might've learned something useful. Let's go find Rosa."

Rosa was indeed in the greenhouse, gathering up the bottles of the ingredients they had already tracked down, her face lined with worry.

"There you are," she said, relieved. "I thought we should take these with us, just in case. Any luck? Please don't worry if you didn't—"

"We got it," Milo announced. "Alessia was amazing—she managed to convince Robin that the arrow should be used for charity, and then persuaded him to give it to us, via Friar Tuck."

"Sounds like quite the performance," Rosa said, and Alessia gave a little bow, which broke through Rosa's worry and prompted a smile. "Okay, we're doing well, team. We have all the ingredients now apart from the lost property item, which we're on our way to get. And then there's just tackling the issue of the Records, but I think that between us and the Pages family we'll be able to work it out. Are you ready to go straightaway? Do you need anything to eat?"

"We've just eaten," Milo said. "Again. There was a feast."

"It was crucial to the plan that we eat it," Alessia said.

"I'm sure." Rosa grinned. "So, to the Quip?"

"Are we leaving Lina here?" Milo asked tentatively.

"We can't bring her with us," Rosa said. "Not only is she exhausted by her trip, but I really don't think it's wise to let her on the Quip, I'm afraid."

"You think she'd try and steal it," Milo said sadly.

"I don't think it's outside the realm of possibility," Rosa replied. "Now, I must admit, despite everything, I'm excited to have my first proper journey onboard. Let's get our things together and set off."

Milo and Alessia headed up to their cozy bedroom cabin to gather the few things they had with them, while Rosa ensured they had the ingredients they'd gathered so far, as well as ointment and gauze for Alessia's ankle.

"I wish we could stay here longer," Milo said as he stuffed his belongings into his backpack.

"Maybe we'll get to come back when everything is fixed," Alessia said. "I hope so."

With a backpack each, the three of them headed back down to the base of the treehouse and through the trees to where the Quip was hiding by the lake.

"So, you'd not traveled on it at all?" Alessia asked Rosa in surprise.

"No," Rosa answered. "Yesterday was the first time I even stepped foot onboard. I must admit I am wary to leave the treehouse for more than the occasional bookwander or grocery trip—even before I had Lina with me. And while Horatio and I had a mutually beneficial working relationship, I never fancied being subject to where he wanted to drive the Quip. I fancy I am in safer hands with you as the Driver, Milo."

Once the three of them were onboard, Milo got out the Driver's whistle and imagined the ground floor of Pages & Co., fixing it firmly in his mind as he blew the whistle and felt the Quip respond to the instruction. It wasn't a long journey by regular rail tracks, so it would be even quicker onboard the Quip. Milo was fairly confident there'd be enough book magic in the

Quip's engine, but he wanted to make sure, especially as it was Rosa's first trip. He wanted to live up to the faith she had in him as the Driver.

"I'd love to see how it works," Rosa said when he told her he was just popping to check on the fuel, so the three of them stepped over the gap between the carriages and squeezed into the engine cab. Rosa watched in fascination as Milo took some of the charged wooden orbs and rolled them into the engine, where they caught fire and started to spark and burn.

"It looks just like when you turn things into pure imagination in books," Alessia pointed out.

"It's essentially the same process, I would think," Rosa replied. "But I'm curious: How do you get the imagination into the balls to begin with?"

"It's easy," Milo said. "In fact, we're starting to run a little low, if you want to help. It's how Horatio used to charge people for using the Quip."

"Another reason I was wary to come onboard," Rosa said.

"You didn't want to pay?" Alessia asked curiously.

"Not that—I just wasn't sure exactly what systems Horatio might have set up to extricate someone's ideas and imagination."

"But they're not something you can use up," Milo pointed out.

"That's true," Rosa said. "Yet I am protective of my own mind, and I'm sure you won't be offended or surprised to hear that I never trusted your uncle, Milo."

"But you can trust me, I promise," Milo said.

"I know." Rosa smiled. "Go on then, if you're happy this is safe and I'm not having anything extra taken without my consent."

"We can use yours straightaway," Milo said. "It can go right into the engine, and then you'll know there's nothing Horatio can do with the orb charged with your ideas."

"That sounds like a good plan," Rosa said. "And I *am* curious."

"Great." Milo grinned, leading them back to the office, where he took out a fresh orb made of normal wood. "Horatio takes a record of everyone who travels on the train and that they've paid, but let's skip that bit."

"Thank you," Rosa said, sitting on the chair Milo gestured toward. He pulled out an hourglass filled with black sand from inside his uncle's desk and set it on the top where they could all see it.

"Okay, so it's really easy," he said, handing her the orb. "You just hold it tight and imagine whatever you'd like, and when it's done the hourglass will—oh, that's strange." He had looked at the hourglass to show Rosa, and the sand was already all at the bottom. "I must've put it the wrong way round." He picked it up and turned it round, but the sand immediately fell back through, as if it were falling through a huge chute, not a tiny hole in the glass. He wasn't even sure how it was physically possible for it to fall through so quickly. He felt flustered and embarrassed at not being able to make it work in front of Rosa and Alessia.

"I'm sorry," he said. "The hourglass must be broken."

"Uh, I don't think it's that," Alessia said, peering closer. "I think it's Rosa. Not that Rosa's *broken*, I mean, but that she's just charging the orbs really, really fast. Here." Alessia picked up a fresh orb. "Go on, turn the hourglass over as soon as I give it to her." Milo did so, and again, as soon as Rosa's fingers touched the orb, the sand whooshed straight through to the other side.

"Ah," Rosa said, looking a little bashful.

"Wow," Milo said, staring at it in wonder. "I've never seen it go that quickly, even for someone like Artemis."

"I do spend a lot of time, really *all* my time, working with imagination," Rosa said. "And I am . . . protected in some ways, and I imagine that supercharges it all a bit."

"Can I ask you a rude question?" Alessia said.

"You can certainly ask," Rosa said. "And I will answer it if I can."

"How old are you?" Alessia asked. "Are you like my father? You've talked of protections and borrowed magic and all of that, and you look young, but then sometimes you don't at all, and you talk like you've lived in the treehouse for a really long time."

"I am not akin to your father in the sense that I do not make or take any potions or suchlike to extend my life, as he does. But you are right that for me it is not quite so simple as the way you two age. The magic I am loaned for my job does have some . . . perks, shall we say. But I am not *so* very much older than I look, I promise you. I have been at the treehouse since I was about your age and became the formal guardian of *The Book of Books* when I was about twenty-five, when my mother, the previous guardian, died."

"How did she die? Sorry, I don't mean to be blunt. I just mean . . . Was it my father?" Alessia asked, looking resigned.

"No, do not worry," Rosa said gently. "It was of natural causes. For many, many generations the Book has been secret, and it took your father hundreds of years to work out that it even existed, and many more to get an idea of what it holds inside. The role of guardian has not traditionally been an arduous one, and was more focused on the study of imagination and bookwandering."

"So, really, you're quite unlucky," Alessia pointed out bluntly.

"You could look at it that way, yes," Rosa said. "Certainly, it has been a little more fraught than I had hoped, but protecting the Book is my job and what I have been taught to do. I am confident we will be able to keep it out of your father's hands."

Milo glanced at Alessia, who looked less sure. Rosa and Milo went back to the engine, where Milo let Rosa roll the charged orb in. The effect was immediate. As soon as the orb caught fire and started to spark with book magic, the Quip shot forward, meaning Rosa and Milo had to grab on to the nearest fixed bits of the train to stay upright. Rosa looked a little embarrassed again at the strength of her own imagination.

"Wow," Milo said. "I bet that means we'll get to Pages & Co. really, really . . ." But he trailed off as the inky darkness of Story started brightening. "I think we're here already," he finished in amazement. "It must be some serious book magic you're borrowing."

Rosa only smiled.

As the expanse of Story melted away, they rolled into Pages & Co., the Quip once again managing to tuck itself unobtrusively round the bookshelves. However, unlike the last time they'd visited, when the shop was closed and empty, this time it was morning, the late summer sun spilling in through the bookshop windows. It seemed the Pages family had not yet closed the shop in preparation for leaving.

And the problem with people who frequent bookshops is that they tend to have very well-developed imaginations.

Which means

that a

large train

arriving in

the middle

of the shop

did not go

entirely unnoticed.

32

Kerfuffle

Milo first realized they had arrived not quite as incognito as they might have hoped when he heard several people screaming.

"That . . . doesn't sound good," Alessia said, her face pale. "Is my father here?"

Rosa checked her watch. "It's only eleven," she said. "We still have seven hours."

"Maybe you ran someone over," Alessia suggested to Milo.

"Of course he hasn't," Rosa said reassuringly, before pausing. "I mean, not that any of us were exactly looking where we were going—should we have stayed in the engine room?"

"No!" Milo protested, before realizing he really had no idea how Horatio avoided running people over. His uncle never stayed in the engine room as they arrived. "I think the Quip knows not to. Anyway, we can worry about the mechanics of it all once we know if we actually *have* run anyone over," he said, throwing the door open to see around twenty people staring at them.

Bewildered and terrified,

they were agog at the train that had woven itself

through the bookshelves. Even more strange was the

fact that there were a handful of people who couldn't

seem to see the train, but had noticed their fellow

shoppers staring at something.

"Uh, hello," Milo said. "Sorry to scare you—is anyone hurt?"

There was silence, and one man shook his head slowly, still not processing what he was looking at. Milo cursed himself for not having thought this through. Of course you couldn't take the Quip into the middle of a bookshop during the day and expect no one to notice. His uncle would never do something like that. The silence was only broken by Archie Pages pushing through the staring group and coming to stand in front of them, hands on his hips. He raised an eyebrow.

"Uh, hello, Mr. Pages," Milo said. "I'm sorry for crashing in like this. I sort of forgot it would be extremely likely for people in a bookshop to be able to see her."

"Quite," Archie said. "I would happily swear to the high levels of imagination in Pages & Co. customers, which is usually an excellent quality to have in a reader. However, you have shown us its potential problems."

"Archie, what—what is going on?" an old lady said, clutching a pile of Regency romances to her chest. "Why is there a *train* in the shop?"

"There's not a train in the shop," a confused man said, looking at the staring people in horror before quickly retreating out of Pages & Co.

"I . . . am not quite sure what to tell you," Archie said, focused on those who could see the Quip. "The conundrum I face is that the truth is the only thing that makes sense, while being the only thing you won't believe. If I told you that this is a train that runs on imagination and has traveled here through layers of the world of Story, how would that land?"

"Come on now, Archie," a man said, the latest cozy-crime hardback in his hand.

"It can travel through stories?!" a little boy said, making a run for the Quip but being held back by his mother.

"It can indeed," Archie said. "Now, to even be able to see it, you all must have a little room in your minds for the impossible to happen. And I'll take suggestions for how else a train would materialize in the shop without causing any damage . . ." There was silence. "Perhaps young Milo here could do something to demonstrate?"

Everyone turned to look at Milo, who felt like he wanted to pass out on the spot.

"Like . . . ?" He looked to Archie for help.

"Like perhaps imagining your way somewhere else?" Archie said with emphasis. "And then, for example, coming back relatively shortly afterward, say an hour or thereabouts? Timing is key after all," he said with a jerk of his head toward the tills, where a large golden clock stood. "And then perhaps we will all be in a better place to carry on?" he finished.

"Right, yes, of course," Milo said. "That makes sense. We'll go get . . . I mean, yes, we'll pop back very soon, and then you'll be ready to close and . . ."

"You're closing early?" the old lady asked. "Is everyone okay?"

"Yes, yes, fine," Archie said. "Just a slight change of plans, family stuff, you know."

"Mr. Pages, hello," Rosa said. "Sorry to invade like this. I just wondered if you had any copies of *The Wizard of Oz* in the shop?"

"Yes, of course we do," Archie said, "ones that are untampered with by anyone."

"Well, actually, that was—" Rosa started but was interrupted by the little boy tugging on Archie's sleeves, asking about the train. "Might you be able to find them for me?" Rosa pushed on.

"Can it wait?" Archie said in surprise. "You will be here long before six, I very much hope?"

"Yes, yes . . . Well, of course," Rosa said. "We'll leave you to it. I'm sure it will be fine for one more hour."

"Perfect," Archie said over a babble of questions from his customers.

"Is Tilly—" Milo started, but Archie cut him off.

"Tilly will be here later," he said firmly.

"Yes, yes, okay," Milo said, hurrying back up the stairs of the Quip, not sure what else to do. The shoppers were talking among themselves, but it was when he saw someone take their phone out and hold it up as if to take a photo that he was finally shoved into action. "We'll just be on our way, sorry for the kerfuffle, everyone. And yes, we'll just show you how this all works and be out of your hair!"

He scurried back into the engine room with Alessia close behind him, and very quickly blew the train whistle, imagining the Underlibrary as precisely and intensely as he could.

Thankfully the Quip seemed to pick up on his urgency, and within seconds, fueled by Rosa's potent imagination, they were on their way again.

"Well, that didn't go to plan." Alessia laughed, somehow maintaining her cool, as she (almost) always did. "Did you see everyone's faces? It's a shame we didn't manage to pick up Tilly."

"That's what you think," a familiar voice said as the door at the end of the carriage opened to reveal Matilda Pages—and her best friend, Oskar Roux.

33

Tales of Bookwandering Bravery

T illy and Oskar were absolutely delighted with themselves.

"We are getting *really* good at stowing away on this train," Tilly said, and Oskar gave her a high five.

"How did you get onboard?" Milo asked in amazement. "And—"

"And who are you?" Alessia interrupted, looking suspiciously at Oskar.

"I'm Oskar," he supplied. "Tilly's

best friend. You may have heard of me in tales of book-wandering bravery. Lost fairy tales? Maps of stories?"

"Never heard of them," Alessia said. "But I guess I do remember Tilly and Milo mentioned you, so if they've vouched for you . . . Hi, I'm Alessia." She stuck out a hand that Oskar shook. "I'm Milo's best friend," she added.

The most treasured kinds of presents are those you didn't even know you wanted but that turn out to be the very thing you most need, and that's just how Milo felt when Alessia, without fanfare, introduced herself as his best friend.

"And this is Rosa," Milo added, completing the introductions. "Who you probably still think of as the Botanist, but that title feels a bit strange and grand now that we know her properly."

Everyone took a moment to say hello to the people they didn't know, and Milo noticed Tilly giving Rosa a once up and down, trying to assess if she could trust her. Rosa was quieter than she usually was, just listening and watching and thinking.

"How *did* you manage to sneak onto the Quip then?" Milo asked Tilly, before Rosa could notice her assessing stare. "And didn't you tell your grandad we were coming?"

"I did, but he refused to just chuck everyone out when the Alchemist said we had until six. He says he won't be intimidated into disrupting Pages & Co. by a threatening megalomaniac. He put a note on the door saying we were closing at noon, and Grandma is getting everything packed and Horatio ready to go—he's still the same, by the way, as safe as can be for an unconscious person. Anyway, I guess we all sort of thought you might turn up a little less noticeably and help us get ready. You should've gone to the top floor where it's quiet."

"How was I supposed to know that?" Milo said in frustration.

"I'm not blaming you!" Tilly said. "It's my fault; I should've thought. You told me in Venice that people don't see what they can't imagine to be true, but I guess, like Grandad said, in bookshops people are good at imagining things."

"I should've thought as well," Milo said. "Horatio told me about this—not in any detail, but I know it's not as simple as the Quip being invisible. I wonder what your grandad will say to everyone."

"Given they've just seen us leave, surely they'll have to believe what he said?" Oskar pointed out.

"That or they'll forget," Rosa said, speaking for the first time. "Those with space in their imaginations will believe in something, however unlikely it is. There might even be some bookwanderers there, or potential bookwanderers, for all we know. And those that just can't quite make space for the impossible will somehow manage to explain it away."

"Anyway," Tilly said, looking at Rosa in fascination, "while you were causing a fuss, Oskar and I seized the moment and slipped onboard at the back, like last time. I knew Grandad wouldn't let me go with you if I asked."

"We found our way through the train like before," Oskar added. "And here we are."

"The way through carriages that are in a straight line?" Alessia said sarcastically.

"Precisely," Oskar said with a grin and a thumbs-up, and Alessia couldn't help but laugh.

"So, the plan is to go to the Underlibrary to find this ingredient you need for the cure to wake Horatio, and then get my family to safety somewhere, long before the Alchemist turns up?" Tilly asked.

"Exactly," Milo agreed.

Tilly was still looking intently at Rosa. "So, where is *The Book of Books*?" she asked, "if it's not with you?"

"I cannot tell you," Rosa said. "I'm sorry."

"Why not?" Tilly pushed. "We're all in danger because of it."

"I know," Rosa said. "But I am concerned that if the Alchemist were to find any of you again, he would go to great lengths to find out what you know. The less information you have, the safer you are. Also, the Book is only protected if it's just me that knows where it is. It is not for the Underlibraries either, or for people like Horatio. And, speaking of Horatio, it is vital we wake him up as soon as possible, as we need what he knows. Despite many of his actions, I am still confident he wants to stop the Alchemist, even if his motivations are not as altruistic as I would wish."

"You mean like the fact he was willing to kidnap me for the Alchemist so he could get his sneaky hands on this book?" Tilly said crossly.

"Well, as we know, Horatio is not an ethical man," Rosa replied. "But he has gone to great lengths to protect Milo and keep the Quip from the Alchemist's hands."

"Wish he felt the same desire to protect *me* as he does a train," Tilly muttered mutinously. "But, whatever, we can all agree he's a . . . complicated man who knows stuff, fine. And regardless of what he knows, we need to wake him up because he's Milo's family."

But they had no more time to discuss Horatio and what he might know or do, as their trip was a very short one, and they had reached the British Underlibrary.

34

Lost Properly

Milo had only been to the British Underlibrary once before, and not in ideal circumstances. Horatio had been contracted to acquire Source Editions that would not be missed so that the evil Underwood twins, who tried to use their tenure in charge of the Underlibrary to secure their own immortality, could destroy them to steal their book magic. They had believed that if something was powerful, then it was valuable and could only be acquired by theft. They never realized that pure book magic was nothing more complicated than imagination. Although Milo could admit that understanding this was one thing, while knowing how to collect and use imagination was considerably more challenging.

"I've imagined us to the Source Library, I hope," Milo said to the others as the Quip stilled. "It's the place I can picture the clearest, although I'm not sure it will look the same as it does in my mind now that Tilly has freed all the Source Editions."

"I still can't believe you pulled that off," Alessia said. "Even if it was just the Source Editions kept here in London, think how many books you made free so that bookwanderers could never risk accidentally ruining an original story—not to mention limiting the books my father can get his hands on."

"Amelia hopes that some of the other Underlibraries might see the appeal and do the same," Tilly said. "She's trying to come up with a way to do it with book magic so she doesn't have to rely on my unusual bookwandering abilities. Or the memory of William Shakespeare."

"It was a curious and impressive idea you had, Tilly," Rosa said. "One that raises questions about the ideal role of the Underlibraries."

"I can't tell if you think that's a good or bad thing," Oskar said.

"It's an interesting thing!" Rosa laughed. "I suppose time will tell! It looks like everything to do with bookwandering is shifting at the moment—it would seem that we're drawing near a moment of crux, with Source Editions being freed and the Alchemist bringing his long-laid plans to a climax. Now, shall we see where Milo has brought us?"

"It can't be worse than a bookshop full of surprised readers." Oskar grinned.

"I think it could be *way* worse than that," Alessia said. "Like a locked dungeon. Or a room on fire. Or we could be perched on top of quicksand."

"I'm pretty sure I wasn't imagining quicksand," Milo said anxiously, but he flung the door open to be sure.

He looked out into a large hall that was the same shape and size as the Source Library but felt like a completely different place. Gone were the rows and rows of steel bookcases filled with books that hadn't been touched for generations. The concrete floor was now laid with plush navy-blue carpet, and the ceiling had been painted a similar dark blue, decorated with the constellations of the night sky. There were still plenty of bookshelves, but they were now made of gleaming wood, not steel, and lined three edges of the room. At one end were rows of wooden desks with individual lamps, and the rest of the space had groups of sofas and armchairs dotted around. Lamps lit the space with a warm glow, and a long table with kettles and coffee machines and plates of biscuits and other snacks ran down one wall.

There were librarians in their Underlibrary cardigans working at the desks, as well as reading and talking in the comfy seating, clutching steaming cups under the night-sky ceiling.

"Okay, so this is different," Tilly said as she came to stand next to him. "This is—"

"It's beautiful," Milo finished. He couldn't believe how different it was from when he'd last been there. The librarians were watching the Quip curiously. Librarians, as a whole, were fairly unflappable people. Good at taking all sorts in their stride and keeping going. They also, of course, had excellently oiled imaginations—especially those who worked at the British

Underlibrary. But a train emerging in their Reading Room couldn't go entirely unremarked upon, and coffees were set down and bookmarks placed firmly along spines as they moved closer.

Milo stepped off the train. "Sorry to interrupt," he said as confidently as he could. "We've just come for something we need, then we'll be out of your way."

Tilly and the others followed him down the steps. The librarians were still watching them, some a little suspiciously, but mainly with undisguised fascination. Milo heard the words *"That's Tilly Pages"* and *"I think those are the kids who defeated the Underwoods"* and realized they weren't totally unknown to the people here.

"Um, have all the librarians who supported the Underwoods definitely left?" Milo whispered to Tilly, worried about who might be learning about the existence of the Quip for the first time. How on earth had Horatio managed to keep it so secret for so long? Milo had been the Driver for less than a week, and already it felt like he'd quadrupled the number of people who had seen the train. His uncle had clearly worked even harder than Milo realized at the time to keep it from the eyes and ears of the Underlibrary—apart from the select few clients he smuggled books for.

"I think so," Tilly replied. "Amelia said that some of the people who didn't stand up to them have been given a second chance, but she's been recruiting lots of new librarians from bookwanderers up and down the country. But of course there are still people here who were always loyal to Amelia and disagreed with the Underwoods like—"

"Is that Milo Bolt I see?" A voice echoed through the Reading Room, and there, striding toward them, was Seb, an Underlibrarian, supporter of Amelia, and loyal friend to the Pages family.

"Hello!" Milo said, pleased to see him. "Sorry for invading you like this."

"Not at all," Seb said. "The pleasure is all mine. You can see our beautiful new Reading Room—this is what we turned the Source Library into—do you approve? It's a space for Underlibrarians to work and study and read and talk, or just have their lunch. And it also has plenty of space for your magnificent . . . train?"

The rustle of paper and clink of coffee cups had started back up in the background, Seb's greeting giving the librarians the final sign they needed that all was well. Nonetheless, Milo made sure to lock the Quip securely.

"It's lovely," Tilly said.

"I don't believe I've had the pleasure of meeting everyone assembled," Seb said, shaking his head and accepting the presence of the Quip, then looking at Alessia and Rosa.

"Oh, sorry," Tilly said. "This is Alessia della Porta. She is . . ." She trailed off, not quite sure how to introduce her.

"She's a friend," Milo supplied. "And this is Rosa . . ." And it was his turn to trail off, realizing he couldn't remember if Rosa even had a surname.

"Hello," Rosa said, stepping forward and shaking Seb's hand. "My name is Rosa Clearwood."

"Charmed," Seb said. "If it's not too impertinent of a question, could I ask what you and four children are doing on the train that's just arrived in our underground Reading Room?"

Rosa laughed. "We were hoping to perhaps speak with Amelia Whisper and to visit the Lost Property Office," she said. "If that's okay?"

"I'm sure it is," Seb said. "But, just to check, do you mean the Lost Property Office, or the Lost *Properly* Office? We have both, you see."

35

Castor and Pollux

"I was right!" Alessia crowed triumphantly. "That's what I wrote down!" she said to the rest of the group.

"She did indeed," Rosa said, smiling. "It was me who insisted it must be lost *property*, and it serves me right for trying to impose the normal rules of things on anything to do with bookwandering and imagination."

"Sorry, are you seriously telling me there's a lost property office *and* a lost properly office?" Oskar asked. He looked at Seb with a mischievous grin. "Are you trying to trip up us dyslexic bookwanderers?"

"I assure you, no," Seb said, looking horrified. "It's no trick; they merely have different purposes. Let me call up to Amelia to let her know you're here, and she can show you."

But before he'd even headed to the desks, the large door to the room opened and Amelia Whisper came in, her shiny black hair tied up in a messy topknot.

"Another illicit mission, Tilly?" she said in a tone of affectionate exasperation.

"Maybe," Tilly said, a little bashfully. "Amelia, this is Rosa, the person we've been calling the Botanist. And she knows about . . ." Tilly paused and looked around her to check they couldn't be overheard. "Well, she's actually the *guardian* of *The Book of Books, and* she's helping us to work out how to turn Alessia's recipe into the cure so we can wake Horatio up."

"Quite the résumé," Amelia said, looking at Rosa, who blushed at the compliment.

"It's an inherited position," she said. "The guardian bit. And the recipe bit is why we're here."

"We were hoping we could see the Lost Properly Office," Milo said. "We think we need something from it."

"Why on earth would you need something from there?" Amelia queried. "That department keeps itself very much to itself. In fact, when I was first an Underlibrarian, I was told to simply let them get on with it and not to ask too many questions!"

"My father's recipe says we need to add something that has been lost properly, for the time taken," Alessia said.

"Ah, now it makes sense," said Amelia.

"Wonderful," Rosa replied.

"Oh, I'm sorry," Amelia backtracked with a slightly embarrassed laugh. "I was being sarcastic. I still am very much in the dark."

"It is quite a . . . poetic recipe," Rosa said. "But I am fairly confident we have interpreted it correctly and it will work. We have almost everything we need."

"That's all very well, but how exactly does one take an item and turn it into medicine?" Amelia asked.

"Rosa knows how to distill things into pure imagination," Milo said, feeling proud to be on a team with someone who knew such things. "We've already collected several things from books."

"This distilling," Amelia asked, "it also lets you take things from books?"

Rosa nodded. "It does, although not in their original form."

"Well, Rosa, I think at some point we should sit down and have a proper chat," Amelia said, her eyes alight. "This all sounds fascinating—I'd love to learn more about it, if you are willing?"

"Oh, absolutely," Rosa said, delighted at Amelia's interest. "Let's get Horatio awake, and the Book and Tilly and her family safe, and then you must come and visit the treehouse."

"That sounds wonderful," Amelia said. "Now let me show you where you're headed."

"Will the Quip be safe here?" said Milo, again making sure the door was locked.

"Of course," said Amelia. "You are friends of the Underlibrary. Your train won't be meddled with, I promise."

They followed Amelia up the stairs from the Reading Room and into the beautiful sweeping main hall of the Underlibrary, with its sky-blue ceiling and seemingly endless grand shelves of books stretching back. Librarians bustled around them, and the air was full of the sounds of cheerful chattering, turning pages, and clacking keyboards. The stairs had led them up through the center of the large circular desk in the middle of the hall, which had the Underlibrary's motto carved onto one side.

"**LEGERE EST PEREGRINARI,**" Milo spelled out. "What does that mean?"

"To read is to wander," Amelia replied. "The motto of all Underlibraries and thankfully one we're a lot more focused on these days. Bookwandering should be about pleasure and learning and adventure; I see our role here to facilitate and protect that, and to keep bookwanderers safe, especially younger ones— not to meddle or dictate what reading or bookwandering means to anyone."

Milo caught Rosa nodding her agreement. The group followed Amelia down the hall and through a door at one end into a corridor. Identical doors, but for the signs on them, stretched out in either direction. Turning left, Amelia led them all the way down to the end of the corridor where two adjacent doors were tucked away. One had a sign that said **Lost Property Office**, and the other read **Lost Properly Office**. Amelia knocked on both, and they both simultaneously swung open to reveal two almost identical men.

"This is Castor," Amelia said, gesturing at the man in the Lost Property Office, who waved in greeting. "And Pollux." She gestured at the man in the Lost Properly Office, who gave a cheery wave. "And they look after many of our lost things."

Castor and Pollux could only be twins, Milo thought. They looked to be in their sixties and wore matching neat suits, Castor's a rich purple and Pollux's burgundy.

"How nice to meet you," Castor said. "Which office are you after today?"

"Lost Properly, please," Milo replied politely.

"Would you mind explaining the difference?" Tilly chimed in.

"Why of course," Pollux said. "Both of us are keepers of lost things—the characters and items that fall off the ends of stories into the Endpapers."

"Including bookwanderers?" Tilly asked, and Milo knew she

was thinking about how she could use the Endpapers to travel to the Underlibraries.

"Thankfully, we lose very few bookwanderers in the Endpapers these days," Pollux said. "But it's a separate librarian who deals with readers; that's all managed by the Endpaper Processing Office—our remit is entirely the fictional."

"Lost Property is my domain," Castor went on. "The things and characters that get nudged off the end of a page. Happens a lot when the endings of books aren't wrapped up neatly. Sometimes there's a character who's not been suitably looked after by their author—I'm sure you know the sort—or has been meddled with by a bookwanderer a little too closely to the end of a book and so tips off the edge of the book."

"But once a reader has finished a book, everything just snaps back to normal, so it's not like the book would be missing anything, right?" Tilly asked. "Especially now that so many of the Source Editions don't exist."

"Quite," Castor said. "The book regenerates itself, so any inanimate objects that have fallen into the Endpapers get left behind here. We use them to study book magic and why inanimate objects seem to be subject to different rules from fictional characters."

"But what about the characters?" Milo asked.

"Obviously, we can't have them wandering around here, so we just pop them back in," Castor explained. "We take them to the very first point where they appear in a book, and after a brief moment of awkwardness, when they see themselves, the two versions of the character simply merge back into who they are at the start of the story."

"So, what ends up in the Lost *Properly* Office?" Alessia asked.

"My brother has the harder job," Castor said.

"You are too generous, brother," Pollux replied. "But things that are lost properly are certainly a little sadder to deal with. I take care of the things that are, well . . . lost properly. They don't belong to anyone or any book anymore, but I keep them safe even if no one will ever need them again, or even miss them."

"I'm not quite sure what you mean," Rosa said politely.

Pollux smiled. "Whenever we bookwander somewhere, we leave a trace of ourselves, and those stories leave a trace in us too. Bookwanderers build up memories and ideas that have been created and curated by being inside the books that built them. These memories and experiences make them who they are as readers, and not just for bookwanderers—all readers. The way you remember exactly where you were when you read something that changed your perspective on something, the time you read the right book at just the right time, when you met a character you fell a little bit in love with on the spot. And then bookwanderers also have the more literal experiences of meeting characters who are beloved to them while they are inside a book, or seeing something truly magical or even terrifying. We leave a trace of book magic in every book we read, a magic that is underestimated. It's how one can stamp bookwanderers, for example, not that I approve of that at all."

And that's also how the Records at the Archive used to work, Milo thought to himself, and he knew the others who had visited the Archive would be thinking the same thing.

"Well, those memories leave a remnant that lingers even after we're gone," Pollux finished. "And that is what is lost properly. But why don't you come and see? It will all become clear."

36

A Sanctuary for Stories

They said good-bye to Castor, who retreated behind his door, and stepped into Pollux's office. The room itself was small. There was nothing in it aside from his desk—no memories or anything that was lost.

"This is simply the reception," Pollux explained, seeing their confused faces. He led them to a door at the back of the room, behind which was a set of stairs that led steeply upward. Following him up to another door, the group watched as Pollux unlocked it and swung it open.

"Welcome to the Lost Properly Office," he said with a small bow as he stepped back to let them in.

The Underlibrary once again amazed Milo. The wood-floored room was not large, but its walls were jammed with cabinets lined with glass bottles of different sizes, each with a colored, sparkling smoky substance. All the smoke was subtly different colors, and some bottles were full to bursting while some had barely a wisp.

"You'll see that some of these are nearly gone," Pollux said. "They dissipate over time, the memories fading with no one to remember them."

"Do you know what memories they are?" asked Oskar, peering at the nearest cabinet. "Or who they belong to?"

"We don't know whose they are," Pollux said. "But that's for the best. And we can't tell precisely *what* they are, as you can't bookwander into a memory. However, if you unstopper one, you do get a sense of what sort of memory it is. You'll get a pang of heartbreak or a whiff of a chocolate factory or a pirate ship. Sometimes you'll even get a whisper of a noise or a conversation. It's quite an intoxicating thing to feel, the echo of someone else's bookwandering memories; I imagine someone could get quite addicted."

"You . . . open them?" said Tilly. "But doesn't that destroy them?"

"They fade away very quickly if they're not bottled, yes," Pollux said. "This isn't a sinister place, to preserve things just for the sake of them. The memories find their way back here, so we keep them as a . . . a form of respect—that's the best way to describe it, I think. But they're also used sometimes as a way to try and understand more about memory and magic. It does no harm to unstopper them and experience an echo of that memory. So, whether the memories are bottled or experienced, they are honored."

It made absolute sense to Milo.

"Here, let me show you," Pollux said, going over to a cabinet and choosing a bottle with barely anything inside, just the suggestion of a curl of sparkling pink smoke. "This is nearly gone, so it will be fairly mild. Don't worry if you don't catch anything at all; it is often just a vestige of an idea you'll feel." He gestured for them to gather round and unstoppered the bottle. The tiny amount of glittering pink smoke drifted out into the air.

Milo was struck by a profound sense of wistfulness and yearning—he was seized by the feeling that there was something he wanted more than anything, although he couldn't put his finger on what exactly that was. There was the gentle scent of Turkish delight on the air, and a creaking, like footsteps on snow, before all of it melted away. The whole thing had only lasted a few seconds, but Milo felt exhausted.

"Wow," he said.

"Did you get it?" Alessia asked, sniffing the air around her as if she was trying to inhale the last moments of the memory.

"I thought I smelled something sweet?" Tilly volunteered.

"It was over so quickly," added Oskar. "It was gone as soon as I felt it."

Milo was confused.

"What did you get, Milo?" Pollux asked, looking curiously at him. "Did you feel something different?"

"Not different, exactly," he said slowly. "Just, *more*, I think? I must have been standing in just the right place for it. I could feel it all like it was me going through it, and I could smell Turkish delight and hear someone walking on snow, and it was like I'd been put into someone . . . else's . . . body." He trailed off as he realized everyone was staring at him. "Is that not normal?" he finished weakly.

"I can't say that it is, young man," Pollux said. "I am very attuned to these memories, and it's taken me years of research to be able to relax my mind in a way that lets them into me the way you've described. You clearly have a natural affinity for this work."

"Milo is very empathetic," Rosa said briskly. "I'm not so surprised that he feels other readers' memories so strongly. They are made of book magic, you say?"

Milo was grateful for Rosa moving the conversation along, although Alessia was still looking at him intently. He avoided her eye contact.

"Of some form, yes," Pollux was explaining. "I hope you don't think it arrogant of me to say that our work here has been a little ahead of some of the prevailing attitudes around book magic. We have long known, for example, that it is much more than something contained in physical books themselves."

"It's a good thing the Underwoods never realized what this place really was about," Oskar pointed out.

"Well, luckily, my brother and I have always been given

a high level of privacy to get on with our work," Pollux said. "As Ms. Whisper knows, we have a degree of autonomy not all departments here get, not to mention the fact they always believed this sort of thing beneath them. All whimsy and sentimentality. It would never have occurred to them that the contents of these bottles were as powerful, if not *more* powerful, than the magic they were stealing."

"So, how do you collect them?" Milo asked. "How do they end up here?"

"Ah, let me show you," Pollux replied, taking them through a door at the far end of the room. There was a chamber on the other side with a great glass sphere at its center, full of wisps and gusts of bookwandering memories dancing around each other. The room was taken up by an elaborate laboratory of glass contraptions drawing memories out of the central sphere and siphoning them into bottles. It was beautiful—each colorful spark a memory of a book.

"Pollux, I think we need to have a chat," Amelia said, looking around her in wonder. "I know you are permitted to have your own space, but I reckon it would be good for both of us to have a . . . catch-up."

"Of course," Pollux said. "I think we will work very nicely together, you and I. I've been doing some . . . experiments for a while now. Book magic calls to book magic—that's why these memories end up at the Underlibrary, I think, because it's a repository of imagination."

"Just like the Archive," Milo whispered to Tilly. "That's why the Archivists ended up there; they left such an impact on the world's imagination."

Tilly nodded her agreement.

"So, I've just created something that intensifies that call," Pollux said, as though it were the simplest thing in the world. "No memory is the same, so they stay distinct and can be siphoned off like this."

"And are these from all over the world?" Rosa asked.

"No, I don't think so," Pollux said. "Although it's hard to know, of course. When we had a Source Library, I thought all the memories to do with the Sources we housed came here, but the Sources have been freed." He paused and smiled at Tilly. "And yet the memories still come. I think they perhaps simply gravitate toward the nearest hub of book magic. There are no doubt many, many memories drawn to other confluences of magic that dissipate over time. You may walk through one without even realizing and get a burst of a feeling or smell, and attribute it to something else altogether."

As Pollux explained, Milo felt a shiver wash over him, his skin breaking out in goose bumps.

"Did you feel that?" he asked Alessia.

"Feel what?" she replied.

"Just a draft, maybe," he said slowly, but then there was something else, another wash of emotions and senses, just like when the bottle had been unstopped in the other room. This one brought the scent of forests and roasting meat and an echo of laughter on the air.

"I think . . . I think I just sensed a new memory arriving," he said to Pollux. "Is that possible?"

"Oh, quite possible," Pollux said. "You are clearly attuned to other bookwanderers and imagination. I sometimes get a shiver of a memory as it arrives."

"I just . . ." Milo looked at Rosa. "What I just felt reminded me of when we were in *Robin Hood* with Lina. That doesn't mean anything, does it?"

"No," Rosa reassured him. "I'm not sure you'd be able to pinpoint the exact book from the memory." She looked to Pollux for confirmation.

"It's unlikely," he said. "You rarely get enough specifics to know, unless it's an extremely unique situation. Does *Robin Hood* have some significance to you?"

"I just worried that . . ." Milo shook his head. "Never mind, you're right; it could have been a memory from so many other different books or people." Still, it sat uneasily with him, and he struggled to keep his worries about what Lina was getting up to at the treehouse at the back of his mind.

"But, whichever book they come from, what do you even *do* with them?" Alessia asked, ever focused on the practical, scientific side of things.

"I keep them until they are gone," Pollux said. "They fade away naturally even when bottled, and so I give them somewhere to exist until they are worn out. Each one is a moment that meant something true and real to a reader. The Underlibrary is about more than rules and regulations; I believe, if you'll permit me, Ms. Whisper, that it's a sanctuary for stories and for readers. And so is the Lost Properly Office."

"It's almost like a very beautiful graveyard," Alessia said.

"I prefer to think of it as a memorial," Pollux replied.

As they made their way back into the room of cabinets, the adults talking at the front, Milo, Alessia, Tilly, and Oskar had a brief moment to themselves.

"I wonder if this is all rooted in the same stuff as our comfort-blanket characters," Milo mused out loud. "I wonder what my reading memories would feel like for someone else."

"I was thinking something similar," Tilly said. "I reckon it would be the things that are at the core: *Anne of Green Gables* for me—the wind in the trees, Anne's laughter, the smell of the crisp autumn air."

"Mine would be *Alice in Wonderland*, I think," Alessia said, getting an approving glance from Tilly. Milo realized he didn't really know who Alessia's comfort-blanket characters were, but Alice made a lot of sense—forthright and clever and a little bit strange, just like Alessia. "It would smell of roses, and the taste of the 'EAT ME' cake would be in the air," she went on. "That's what I think of when I think of Alice. The sound of flamingos squawking in the background."

"I'm not sure what my memory would be," Oskar said.

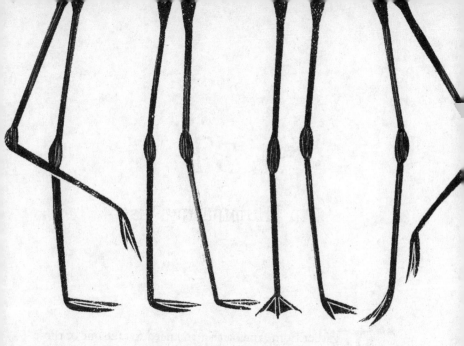

"I think the bookwandering adventure that will make me who I am is yet to come. Although our first trip to Treasure Island would be up there, Tilly. The smell of pirates and fish, delightful!"

"Mine would be *The Railway Children*," Milo said, certain of his answer. "Fresh air and train whistles and a feeling of being exactly where you're supposed to be."

37

An Illuminating Visit

"I gather from Amelia that you need to take one of these with you," Pollux said as the group recongregated. "I'm afraid there's no reliable way of knowing what a memory is, although the colors can sometimes give you a clue as to their mood. Sometimes the way they move gives you some hints as well. I'd recommend you choose a fresh one, where the bottle is still full and lively, to give you the best chance of success at distilling it somehow. Perhaps you should take a few to be sure. Please, feel free to select what you want."

"May we each choose one?" Rosa asked.

"Of course," Pollux said. "They have no purpose here beyond respect and research—I like to think that the ones you choose won't be lost properly anymore but will have served some greater purpose. Another worthy way to honor them."

Milo walked up and down the cabinets, hoping one of the memories would stand out to him. Eventually he decided on a deep-foresty-green one that was nosing its way around its bottle in a curious but gentle sort of way. Alessia held a bottle that had a delicate gray memory hanging in a misty cloud. Oskar's was bright orange and bumping into the sides of the bottle with vigor, and Tilly had chosen one that was periwinkle blue, the same color as the Pages & Co. sign. Milo did not see what Rosa had chosen as she had already put it into her backpack. She had stayed quieter than Milo was used to: less cheery and chatty than usual but watchful instead, letting the children take the lead on the conversation a lot of the time.

"Do you have what you need?" Amelia asked. "If you do, I was hoping I could catch a lift back to Pages & Co. on the Quip so I can help there. And, Rosa, I'd love to speak to you further about *The Book of Books* and what you know of the Alchemist's plans. It will affect us all if he manages to take control of more books and more imagination."

"I'd love to speak further," Rosa said. "But naturally it's up to Milo about the Quip."

"Oh yes, of course you can," Milo said awkwardly, feeling unqualified to be the one deciding whether an Underlibrarian traveled onboard the Quip.

"Thank you," Amelia said. "Shall we, then? Thank you, Pollux, for an illuminating visit."

Pollux gave a little formal bow of acknowledgment and then shepherded them toward the door.

"A pleasure to see you, Ms. Whisper," he said. "And how

delightful to meet the rest of you. Do let me know how you get on with this potion you are concocting—I would be very happy to hear my memories have helped, and curious to know more about how they worked. I have a feeling we will speak again, sooner rather than later."

"Thank you for your help," Rosa said.

"Thank you," the others chorused as the door to the Lost Properly Office shut behind them.

Rosa checked her watch.

"Nearly one o'clock," she said with a nod. "Plenty of time to get back to Pages & Co."

Soon they were back at the Quip, which had stayed nestled in the beautiful new Reading Room. Amelia had never been onboard before and was fascinated. Milo was entertained to see that Rosa was enjoying explaining it to her. As they got closer to waking Horatio up, Milo had started thinking more and more about what Horatio would want to do about the Quip. Who would the Driver's whistle work for? Milo was realistic about his uncle, and he couldn't imagine a scenario in which Horatio would be happy to relinquish the Quip to his twelve-year-old nephew. He knew Horatio would want to get back to book smuggling as soon as they had dealt with the Alchemist—if they managed to actually deal with the Alchemist, that was.

"Can I get anyone a cup of tea or anything?" Milo asked once they were all sitting at a table in the dining car, wanting to make sure everyone felt comfortable.

"Oh, yes please, I'd love one," Alessia said immediately.

"I think Milo could do with a break from worrying about all of us," Rosa said. "Milo, why don't you just focus on getting us back to Pages & Co. for now? Let's not risk any unexpected detours."

So, Milo did as he was asked, closing his eyes and imagining the (totally free of customers) ground floor of Pages & Co. He blew the Driver's whistle and off they went.

"Come on, we can do the drinks," Oskar said brightly. "I'm sure between us we can work it out." He stood up, but no one else moved. "Alessia?" he prompted.

"Excuse me?" she said, looking affronted. "Were you talking to me? I think I'm needed—I am the Alchemist's daughter after all."

"We'll only be gone a little bit," Oskar said. "Let's embrace our sidekick natures."

"Speak for yourself," Alessia said, but she pushed herself up, and Milo was sure he caught a smile on her face.

"Let me get this straight," Amelia said. "The Alchemist is after *The Book of Books*, which he believes to be at your treehouse, Rosa—but he's incorrect?"

Rosa nodded.

"So, where is it?" Tilly asked again. Rosa looked awkward, and Milo noticed Amelia looking at her carefully.

"You can't say," Amelia said. "Because it keeps us safer if we don't know. It has to all be on your shoulders . . ."

"Quite." Rosa nodded.

"I can see why they put you in charge." Amelia smiled. "Can you tell us anything about how it is being protected, though?"

"It is almost impossible to find without clues," Rosa said. "It is imperative that the Alchemist doesn't find it, but the safety of Tilly and the Pages family is more important, as he can get to them in a way I truly believe he cannot get to the Book. Not without someone telling him where to start, which is why I cannot tell anyone. I—I will tell you that it is hidden inside a book, as you might have guessed or wondered. This overwhelmingly reduces the chance of anyone being able to bring it out, but between Tilly and the Alchemist, that probability can never be zero. And, of course, if the Anonymous Reader were to enter the right book, they could read *The Book of Books*'s contents and memorize much of it, or copy down sections, if they were so inclined. But it is also guarded by someone in the book—someone who knows a great deal more about imagination than anyone else."

"A fictional character?" Milo asked. "Or a someone like the Bookmarks my uncle uses, or the man the Alchemist used to keep the poison cabinet guarded?"

"It's not quite as simple as either/or," Rosa said. "The thing is that . . ."

But she was interrupted by a great, *shuddering crash*, as if they had collided with something **extremely solid.**

38

Stuck in Story

osa and Amelia *were slammed into the side* of
the table, and Milo and Tilly were thrown back
against the seats as ripples of impact from
the crash *ricocheted* down the train. Milo leaped
to his feet: he could feel in his bones that the Quip had been
damaged, but he had no idea if it was purely physical or something deeper. What had he done wrong? There was no time for
him to mess up.

"Oskar!" Tilly shouted.

"And Alessia," Rosa said, pulling herself up, grimacing in
pain.

"We're okay, we're okay!" Oskar said, stumbling back from
the kitchen. "Are you all?"

"Yes, everyone's in one piece. What on earth happened?"
Amelia asked.

Milo had no idea; he'd never felt anything like it before

in all his years onboard the Quip. He rushed to the door and nimbly climbed up the ladder to the top of the train, where he ran to the front. They seemed to be on the cusp between Story and the real world. He could see the street the bookshop was on, but as though through a dark glass, as though they were being held suspended between Story and the busy streets of London.

"What's going on?" Tilly asked as she appeared behind him. "Why can't we get home?"

"I don't know," Milo said. "I'm going to try again and see if I can ask the Quip to go as slowly as possible."

He climbed down into the engine room and checked there was enough book magic burning—it was at the perfect level. He put one gentle hand on the Quip's wall and imagined Pages & Co. as carefully as he could, picturing the cozy fireplace, the tall windows, the shelves and shelves of books, the café at the back, and Archie and Elsie Pages behind the till. He put a hand on the brake to keep the train as slow as he could, willing the Quip to pay attention and go cautiously before he blew the whistle again. The Quip shuddered and tried to move, but it was as though there were an invisible wall in front of them, as though they couldn't quite break through the veil that separated them from getting out of Story.

"Are we stuck in Story?" Tilly asked quietly, sounding as scared as Milo felt.

"I don't know, I don't know," he said. He didn't know what he could do; he let the brake go completely, but still, nothing.

They were just pushing
against a barrier they couldn't
see. "I'm going to try and go somewhere else close by," Milo said. He closed
his eyes and imagined the street outside Pages &
Co.; he would worry about any particularly imaginative
passersby if they got there.

He blew the whistle, and the Quip immediately slid forward as if nothing had happened. The train slipped easily into
the real world and tucked itself among some trees on the far
side of the road, the passersby moving out of the way without
realizing why they were changing course. A few people stopped
in shock, and Milo worried they could see the Quip, but before
long they shook their heads as if to clear a bad idea and carried
on their way, looking slightly puzzled.

"Well, that's good," he said with a sigh of relief as he
climbed down to the path, joining the others in front of the
train. "We're not stuck in Story, at least."

"But what happened?" Amelia asked. "Why couldn't we
get to Pages & Co.?"

"Probably my fault," Milo said. "I maybe
made a mistake with what I told the
Quip to do. I'm still pretty new to all
of this." He desperately wanted

that to be true; he had never wanted something to be his fault more, but deep inside he knew it wasn't that.

Tilly had also clearly felt that something was fundamentally wrong as she was darting across the road to the doors of the bookshop. But as she got to the door, she paused and held out a tentative hand. She reached out slowly and touched something Milo couldn't see, and then a burst of sparking book magic erupted from her fingertips. Lines of book magic spread from where she'd touched, revealing a previously invisible surface domed over Pages & Co., golden threads spiderwebbing out like cracks in glass.

"What on earth is going on?" Oskar breathed.

"This has my father's fingerprints all over it," Alessia said, looking nauseous.

"But it's only one o'clock!" Rosa said, checking her watch desperately.

"Something must have changed," Amelia said. "Does he think Tilly is in there? Is he trying to trap her?"

"No," Rosa said, her face white with fear. "He's worked it out."

"Worked what out?" Milo said slowly.

"He's worked out where the Book is," she said, staring across the road at the bookshop and Tilly desperately trying to get through the barrier. "He knows it's at Pages & Co."

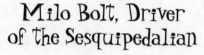

39

Milo Bolt, Driver of the Sesquipedalian

Milo and the others quickly crossed the road to Tilly, who had tears running down her face.

"What's happening?" she sobbed. "Why can't I get home?"

"It's my father," Alessia said, reaching a finger out to gently touch the barrier, sending more sparks into the air.

"Tilly," Milo said urgently, "it's because *The Book of Books* is here—or rather, it's inside a book that's in Pages & Co. Rosa just told us. And the Alchemist must have found out."

"I don't understand how," Rosa said, looking shell-shocked. "I've never told anyone."

"You should have told us!" Tilly shouted, spinning on her heel to face Rosa in anger. "You said you couldn't say to keep me safe, to keep my family safe, and now look! Does this look safe to you?" She kept banging on the barrier, but it didn't move, just crackled and sparked and sent out more jolts of book magic.

"Can you phone them?" Milo suggested.

"Oh my goodness, I hadn't thought," Tilly said, pulling her mobile out of her pocket and desperately tapping on the screen before holding it to her ear. A few moments later, she let out a great sob.

"Grandad! It's me, Tilly! Are you okay?" She tapped a button to put the mobile on speakerphone so everyone could hear.

"We're okay, Tilly," Archie's tinny voice said. "Are you safe?"

"Yes, I'm with Amelia," Tilly replied quickly.

"Okay, good," Archie said, and Milo could hear the relief in his voice.

"Who's in there?" Tilly asked.

"Just us, thank goodness," Archie said. "Just your mum, your grandma, and me. And Horatio, of course. But we're all safe; we just can't get out."

"I know—I'm trying to get in!" Tilly said.

"You're here?"

"I'm outside!"

And then there was the sound of the phone clattering to the ground, and the door to Pages & Co. swung open to reveal Tilly's grandad. Milo thought that his heart might break watching Tilly and her grandad so close but unable to get to each other. They each put a hand up to the barrier, and their palms met on either side, sending more lines of golden book magic out in a starburst.

"Do you know what's happening?" Archie asked, his voice sounding strange through the barrier, as though he were underwater.

"It's the Alchemist," Rosa said, stepping up to the barrier. "I'm so sorry, Mr. Pages. It is my fault this has happened, and I promise you I will do everything in my power to protect you and the Book."

"The Book?" Archie repeated. "This *Book of Books* that the Alchemist is after?"

"Yes," Rosa said. "It's kept within a book that is in Pages & Co."

"That's nonsense," Archie said. "I think I'd know about such things."

"It has been hidden in this building for a very long time," Rosa said. "It is not supposed to be found or known."

"Well, where is it?" Archie said. "Given that we're now trapped."

"I . . . I cannot tell you," Rosa replied stiltedly. "It must not fall into the hands of the Alchemist."

"What exactly makes it worth all this?" Archie asked in frustration.

"It holds the secrets to the very beginnings and essence of bookwandering," Rosa said. "What is inside gives the reader power over all books, and access to profound magic that would change the world if put in the wrong hands. Mr. Pages, are you able to bookwander? Can you hide in a book you know to be safe, one where the Source Edition no longer exists, where the Alchemist couldn't track you?"

"It doesn't work," Archie said. "We tried as soon as we realized, but whatever is keeping us here is also stopping us from bookwandering."

Rosa slammed her hand on the barrier in frustration, and Milo realized he had barely seen her angry before.

"Have you heard from the Alchemist?" Milo asked.

"No, nothing!" Archie said. "This thing only descended about fifteen minutes ago, after the last customers left. We felt this shuddering, and then when I opened the door to see what was happening, I discovered I couldn't leave. And when I checked the clock I realized it had stopped."

"Why would he do this and yet not be here?" Rosa said to herself.

"Might he have sent us a message?" Milo thought aloud. "Via the Quip?"

"Go and check!" Tilly shouted.

Milo pelted back across the road, Alessia in tow, and straight to the postbox in the office of the Quip. He yanked open the drawer, and there inside was another letter with the same thick parchment and ink Milo now recognized as the Alchemist's.

"I should give it to Tilly," Milo said, holding it up to Alessia.

"But this one is addressed to you," Alessia said. Milo turned the envelope round and actually read the address to see that Alessia was right. It wasn't addressed to Tilly but to him:

Milo Bolt, Driver of the Sesquipedalian

Milo froze with the letter in his hand. What did the Alchemist want with him? It must be to do with Horatio and the contract—he was still after the Quip.

"If your father had the Quip and the Book, I'm guessing he could do some pretty powerful stuff," he said slowly to Alessia.

"I dread to think," Alessia replied. "But you should probably see what he has said. Now."

"Right," Milo said, still not quite able to open the letter.

"Oh, come on," Alessia said, grabbing it from his hand and

unsealing it. She pulled out a sheet of thick paper and flung it back at him. "There. Or should I read it?"

"No," Milo said, taking the paper and making himself read the words.

Milo,

It is time for us to talk directly, and I am optimistic that you may be more amenable than your friends. While your uncle flew too close to the sun in his attempts at double-dealing, I hope you will have learned from your time in his care that his approach to business and opportunities was pleasingly free from the tedious idea of ethics. He certainly saw the world in shades of gray, something I have always respected in a person. I wonder how you see the world, Milo?

You will perhaps have already realized that circumstances have changed. I have come into new knowledge that supersedes my previous generous offer. It became clear to me that Matilda would not be contacting me before my deadline and that your collective actions have made a mockery of my civil attempts at negotiation.

It was not difficult for me to follow where you had taken the Quip; it leaves such great tracks of book magic in its wake, if you know how to see these things. And so, I find myself writing this from a beautiful treehouse in Northumberland, full of the most interesting work. The Botanist was clever enough to ensure there were no copies of *The Wizard of Oz* in her quaint treehouse, but I was able to get close enough and then follow the Quip's tracks.

I have had the pleasure of encountering an old acquaintance and business partner, your grandmother. Lina has been ever so kind as to tell me some of the things she has learned while living here. I always did admire her ability to collect knowledge and leverage, and she has proved most helpful, despite needing some encouragement.

All of this is to say, Milo, that I know the Book is at Pages & Co. And so, I have placed it under my, shall we say, protection. And I will tear that shop apart to find the Book, however long it takes me. And when I have found it, I will collect Matilda, who will not see her family again if she does not bring the Book to me and open it.

By the time you see this, I will have left the treehouse, so do not rush on my account. But Lina will remain, and you may wish to rush on her account.

Yours,

Geronimo della Porta

Milo flung the paper at Alessia and yelled across the street as she read: "Rosa! We need to go. Now."

Rosa looked up and saw his face, immediately running across the street to the Quip.

"What?" she said urgently.

"He got to Lina," Milo said. "Alessia has the letter—you can read it on the way. But it was her who told him about Pages & Co., and that we were never planning on helping him at all, and it sounds like he's . . . hurt her or something awful." His voice was shaking; he couldn't think too much about what they would find when they got back.

"But . . . she doesn't know," Rosa said in desperate confusion.

"Clearly, she does!" Milo shouted, sharper than he meant. "And we need to go. Are the others staying?"

"If the Alchemist is coming here, we need to get Tilly and Oskar away," Rosa said.

"She won't leave her family," Milo replied.

Amelia, Tilly, and Oskar joined them on the other side of the street.

"What's going on?" Tilly asked.

"We have to get back to the treehouse now," Rosa said.

"I'm not leaving," said Tilly immediately, as Milo knew she would.

"You can't stay here—it's not safe," Milo insisted. "He's coming."

"And you want me to just leave my family here waiting for him to come?" Tilly said, crying.

"We can't help them from here," Rosa said. "But there might be something we can do from the treehouse. And you're just a sitting duck waiting here, and you have nowhere to sleep or eat."

"I don't care!" Tilly cried.

"You have to let her make her own decision!" Oskar said, standing protectively by Tilly's side.

"Tilly," Amelia intervened, kneeling down in front of her and taking her hands. "You need to go with Rosa; you need to stay safe. They'll need your brains and your courage to fix this. I will stay here, I promise. I will sit in that coffee shop opposite Pages & Co. and I will watch it. I will stay on the phone with your grandparents, and if anything changes I will call you immediately, okay?"

"None of this is okay!" Tilly said.

"I know," Milo said. "None of it is okay or fair! But the faster we get away from here, the faster we can work out what to do. You can't help them from here, but you can from the treehouse."

"Do you promise?" Tilly said, looking up at Rosa. "Because it seems to me like this is all your fault. They're trapped there because there's a book hidden there they had no idea about."

"I didn't hide it there," Rosa said. "But that's beside the point, I know. I'm sorry I didn't tell you, but I promise you I'm not the enemy. This is the Alchemist's fault, and we must get to the Book before he does."

"How are we going to do that when it's in *there*?" Alessia said. "On the other side of the barrier?"

"There is one route," Rosa said. "A longer path, but perhaps our only option now. However, we *must* get going. We need to find Lina, and we need to get the Book."

"Okay," Tilly said, sounding defeated, and she let Milo take her by one arm and Oskar by the other, and lead her onto the train. She gave Amelia a nod and then went into a corner and called her grandad to tell him where she was going. Milo focused as hard as he could, trying to crowd out thoughts of Lina and Horatio and Tilly's family, and just imagine the treehouse.

And as if she could sense the urgency, the Quip wriggled to life instantaneously, and they were off.

40

The First Bookwanderer

Tilly's phone lost signal as soon as they were in the realm of Story again, and she joined them.

"Sorry I said this was all your fault," she said quietly to Rosa.

"You don't need to apologize for anything at all," Rosa said. "Not even slightly. You're dealing with a level of pressure and worry that no one should experience, let alone someone your age. And I am struggling to know whether I did the right thing in not telling you where the Book was, given what has happened."

"You had no way of knowing that Lina knew," Milo pointed out. "Although how did she find out?"

"I really am not sure," Rosa said. "And that is worrying me a great deal."

"Is it written down anywhere at the treehouse?" Alessia asked.

"Well, yes, I suppose so," Rosa said. "I have private records to do with my job as the Book's guardian. There's not exactly a sticky note with its location, but there are of course references and notes about Pages & Co."

"In that case I'm not sure it's so difficult to work out how she knew," Alessia said.

"But those records are locked away, and I made it very clear that Lina was not to go into the greenhouse without me."

"Much as I wish my grandmother were a different person," Milo said, "I'm not sure from what I know of her that asking her not to go somewhere and locking something away would make that much of a difference if there was something she wanted to find out."

"It would seem I have been very foolish," Rosa said.

"Or just very naive," Alessia said, patting Rosa on the arm as if that were a comforting thing to say.

"The thing is, though," Oskar said firmly, "it doesn't really matter anymore how she found out—or rather that's something to deal with later. Because Tilly's family is stuck inside of Pages & Co., and the Alchemist is going to do anything to find the Book."

"We need to know how much Lina knows, and how much she's told him," Rosa said. "It's vital we understand the best way to protect both Tilly's family and the Book. I am sure it will become clear to the Alchemist that your family had no idea the Book was hidden there."

"Why *is* the Book hidden there?" Milo said. "It seems a bit, well, you know . . ."

"Random," Oskar supplied. "I think that's probably the word you're looking for."

"It's not so unlikely if you understand the history of Pages & Co.," Rosa said. "We don't have much time before we get back to the treehouse, but I'll tell you as much as I can. Tilly, how much have you been told about your family's shop?"

"That it's been in my family for a long time," Tilly said slowly. "Grandad always said that we come from a long line of booksellers—that it's in my blood."

"He's absolutely right," Rosa said. "Did you know there's been a bookshop run by your family in London since the printing revolution in Europe?"

"What?!" Tilly said. "When even was that?"

"Johannes Gutenberg introduced the movable-type printing press to Europe in the fifteenth century," Alessia said casually.

"How do you even know that?" Milo said in amazement.

"I know a lot about books," Alessia said. "I mean, only child, evil father, lots of books about books around to pass the time."

"Oh right," Milo said awkwardly. Somehow he kept divorcing Alessia from her father in his brain. She was so sarcastic and confident that it was easy to forget what she must be dealing with now that she was fighting against her father. He reminded himself that she used sarcasm and confidence to cover up all sorts of feelings that must be much more complicated.

"Anyway," Oskar said pointedly, "we were talking about Pages & Co.?"

"Yes, so your family have been booksellers of sorts for a very long time indeed," Rosa said to Tilly.

"Since the fifteenth century?" Tilly asked.

"Even longer than that," Rosa said.

"But you just said—"

"That's when Pages & Co. was established as a shop," Rosa said. "Actually, it was a printer and shop then, but now isn't the moment for a lesson on the history of bookselling. And of course it wasn't where it is now at that point either. It moved there in the 1800s, if I remember correctly. It is more accurate to say that your family have been purveyors and protectors of stories for a very long time."

"No wonder the Alchemist thinks you're the Anonymous Reader," Alessia said.

"It certainly is an easy theory to believe," Rosa said. "Especially given what the Alchemist prioritizes and values. The thing I am hoping he does *not* know about is the extra layer of protection I mentioned. He clearly suspects the Book is inside another book, and that is another reason why he wants

Tilly—he knows she can take items out of books. In his mind, all of it adds up to Tilly being the Anonymous Reader, and therefore the one who can unlock *The Book of Books* for him. But I very much doubt he has factored in that within the book where it is hidden, there is also someone who protects it—the man who bequeathed the legacy of housing the Book to Tilly's family so many generations ago. The first bookwanderer."

"Who is he?" Milo asked. "Do we know him? Does Tilly?"

"You will have heard of him," Rosa said. "His name is Merlin."

41

Myths and Legends

There was a stunned silence.

"As in . . . *the* Merlin?" Tilly said. "King Arthur, Knights of the Round Table, Sword in the Stone Merlin?"

"The very same," Rosa said. "He was the first bookwanderer, and he is the protector of the Book."

"Does that mean *The Book of Books* is inside a book of King Arthur myths?" Milo breathed in amazement.

"It is indeed," Rosa said. "A very particular version of them, which has been hidden with the Pages family for over a thousand years."

"But that's before the printing press," said Alessia.

"Yes," Rosa said. "But it is not a printed book. It is a bound, handwritten manuscript."

"This is . . . a lot to take in," Tilly said.

"I still have a few questions," Alessia added.

"I'm sure you do," Rosa said. "But we can tackle them as we go; we need to use every moment we have. Milo, are we nearly back to the treehouse?"

Milo paused and put a hand on the Quip's wall.

"Yes," he said, feeling her starting to slow. "Only a few minutes to go I would say."

"The key question I have, though," Alessia insisted, "is this: If this book is in Pages & Co., how on earth do we get to it? Not sure if you noticed the giant invisible wall of book magic stopping us from getting in?"

"I did," Rosa said. "But there are other ways, if you know how."

"We could use your father's potion?" Tilly suggested. "The one we made for Artemis that let her escape—isn't that what your father uses to bookwander without a book?"

"I don't know how it works, though," Alessia said, clearly frustrated at the limits of her own knowledge. "It's one thing making the potion, but I've no idea how you imagine yourself into a specific copy of a book."

"Don't worry, Alessia," Rosa said. "I'm sure you could work it out if we need it, but Merlin is not bound by the pages of just one book."

"I'm confused," Oskar said. "Is Merlin real or fictional? How can he be a bookwanderer?"

"You are all friends with Tilly," Rosa pointed out. "You have seen how it is not always so clear-cut as that. Merlin is of both worlds; he is of our world and of Story. He exists outside the usual way of things. He is the source of bookwandering magic as we understand it. Merlin is made of many myths and legends, real and imagined tales."

"So, we just . . . call him up? Email him?" Oskar suggested.

"Not far off," Rosa said. "We will let him know we need him, and we will go and meet him. I hope. I have never had to do this before."

"I really hope this works," Tilly said.

"Me too," Rosa replied as the Quip emerged among the Scots pine trees by the lake.

42

A Deal with the Devil

Even with all the worry, Milo managed to find some small, if complicated, slice of pleasure from watching Tilly and Oskar get their first look at the treehouse as they slipped through the wall of trees that hid it from passing eyes. It was twilight as they arrived, and strings of fairy lights were strung from tree to tree, illuminating the various cabins and platforms, and soft light spilled from the library windows.

"Welcome," Rosa said, running her hands through her hair. "I'm sorry that it's not under more pleasant circumstances. Now, we must find Lina first. Milo, will you take Oskar and look in the library? Alessia, take Tilly and check Lina's room, and I'll check the greenhouse. Whoever finds her, just yell as loudly as you can, please."

She took off running up the stairs, and Milo gestured for Oskar to follow him to the library, scared of what they might find. However complicated Lina was, he wasn't ready to lose her yet. He pulled the door to the library open, but there was no one in the main hall.

"Lina?" he shouted. "Are you here?"

"Is that . . . Milo?" a voice croaked from somewhere above them. Milo's heart squeezed as he followed the voice up a ladder to one of the snug cubbyholes full of books. Lying on a beanbag, in horrible juxtaposition to the coziness and warmth of the library, was his grandmother. She had no obvious injuries, but she was gray-faced, breathing hoarsely and barely holding her head up. He froze the second he saw her, a spell only broken by Oskar's gasp of horror.

"Oskar, go get the others," Milo said as he thawed, tripping over his feet as he ran to his grandmother and knelt beside her. He picked her hand up gently.

"Are you okay?" It felt like a silly question as soon as it left his lips.

"Not especially." Lina smiled weakly. "He gave me something—I don't know what it was, but it has not agreed with me, as you can see. I do not think there is anything to be done for me now. This path was set a long time ago, and fixed by the Alchemist's potion. I am glad I could cling on until you returned, though, Milo."

"Was it some kind of truth serum or something?" Milo asked, desperate for there to be a reason she would have given up Rosa's secret. "He could make one of those, right?"

"I wish I could say it had been," Lina said. "But no, I think that I've become merely a pawn in his game—a warning to you all of how serious he is. Perhaps I have been . . . naive . . . to think he thought of me . . . differently from others he entangled in his schemes."

"But how did you even know the Book was at Pages & Co.?" Milo asked.

"I was not content to simply exist here at the mercy of Rosa," Lina said, stopping to cough painfully. "I had dreams of discovering her secrets and perhaps being able to claim the Quip back—to come to some new agreement with the Alchemist, to live the life I ought to have had."

"What?" Milo said, dropping her hand. "You snooped around just to try and get the Quip back?"

"Milo, you do not know the life I have lived," Lina said, clutching for his hand. "To have experienced endless freedom just to end up essentially a prisoner in some corner of the countryside."

"It was to keep you safe!" Milo said. "After what you did, this is a luxury! I would *love* to live here."

"It is not enough," Lina breathed. "I deserve more. He could have given me more if I had played my cards better."

"Why did you trust him? Why would you sell us all out for someone like that?" Milo said, tears flowing.

"He's the only one with the power to help me get back my train, to get back what I deserve," Lina said. "Milo, think of what you and I could've created on the Quip with the things

I've learned from Rosa! Sometimes . . . a deal . . . with the devil is worth it."

"Clearly, this isn't worth it!" Milo half shouted, half sobbed. "What have you done?"

"I regret only that I won't see Horatio again." Lina coughed.

"We were working to wake him up!" Milo said. "If you'd just—just *not*! Why would you have told the Alchemist we weren't going to help him? And now who knows if we'll be able to wake Horatio? We can't get the cure to him anyway! And because of what you did, we don't have time to work out what to do for the record of the reader ingredient for the cure now that the Archive Record is no use!"

"Milo," Lina said, pulling him close to her with all the strength she had left. "The record of a reader is not in some papers or a ledger, it's in the stories that build us, that make us who we are, and in the stories we leave behind." She paused to try and catch her breath. "You do not need that book to have the record of your uncle. You just need to know the stories that made him who he is."

"I have no idea what they are!" Milo cried. "He never talked to me! No one ever did! I barely know who *I* am."

"You are not so different, it seems," Lina stammered. "You both always knew that the railway was full of enchantment."

"What?" Milo said. "What are you saying? Why do I know that phrase?"

"I couldn't keep him out of *The Railway Children* as a boy,"

Lina said. "He was always off with those kids. If any book made him, it's that one."

"But that's *my* favorite book," Milo said in shock.

"So I've heard," Lina replied, coughing hard once more.

At that point the door to the library banged open again. Within a few moments, the cubbyhole was crowded with people, but Milo felt as though he and his grandmother were the only ones there.

"Lina, what did you do?" Rosa whispered.

"I always knew I wasn't one to fade away," Lina gasped. "I always wanted an ending that would make a good . . . story."

And with that she collapsed backward against the beanbag, and Milo felt her hand go limp in his. And for the briefest of moments, Milo thought he caught the scent of bonfires and book magic on the edge of the breeze.

43

The Anonymous Reader

There was silence. And then Milo heard Alessia start to cry.

Milo found his own tears had stopped now that his grandmother was gone, and he felt empty. He had just met his only other living family member, and now she was gone—and gone like this, used as a pawn by the Alchemist after she had betrayed them all. Right until the end, she had prioritized what she wanted over everyone else. Whatever he was feeling was not so straightforward as grief.

He felt a gentle hand on his shoulder and looked up to see Rosa. He stood and without thinking fell into her. She wrapped her arms round him and bundled him up in the tightest hug he had ever been given. He felt his breathing calm and his head stop buzzing, and he pulled back from Rosa. She gave him a querying look, and he nodded his head to show he was ready to keep going.

"We can't leave her here," Milo said.

"Of course not," Rosa said. "There is a bookseller who lives close by, a bookwanderer and someone I trust. I will call them, and they will come and look after her and make sure everything is in order."

Milo nodded his agreement as Rosa leaned forward and covered Lina with a blanket so she looked simply as though she were an old woman, fallen asleep among the books.

"Milo," Rosa said. "I hate to ask this of you when this is so fresh and raw—I can't imagine how you must be feeling—but did she tell you anything we need to know?"

"She said that she always wanted to learn more about what you were doing so she could get the Quip back," Milo said, not able to look at Rosa. "She told the Alchemist our plans and where the Book was just to get leverage. She thought he would help her get the train, and help her escape, but once he had what he needed, he poisoned her—to send a message to us."

Tilly looked as though she was about to be sick, she was so scared.

"And also . . . she told me how to finish the cure. I think," he added. "She said what we could use instead of the Record—I know what the last ingredient is. It's in *The Railway Children*."

Tilly gave him a look, knowing what that book meant to him.

"I think what she was trying to tell me was that a Record is no more complicated than a physical token of someone as a reader. Really, it's just a list of the books that made them who they are. So, if you know a person, and you know the book that is at their core"—he looked at Tilly—"their comfort-blanket book, that's the true record of a reader, a marker of who they are. And Horatio's is . . . well, the same as mine." He could feel more tears on his cheeks, but he could also feel Alessia and Tilly and Rosa and Oskar around him like a protective shield.

"But we can't get it to Horatio," Alessia pointed out. "And we don't have time to make the cure."

"Not yet," Rosa said. "But we have everything else we need, and my kit is on the Quip still. We'll get a copy of *The Railway Children* to take with us, and we'll hopefully be able to do . . . everything." She looked exhausted. "We're going to need Horatio in the end. Now, let's go and find the Book. Milo, we don't have far to go, but it is at least half an hour's walk. Can you take us on the Quip?"

"Will I be able to imagine somewhere I've never been?" Milo asked.

"I am hoping I can help with that," Rosa said.

The four children and Rosa headed quickly down the stairs and back to the Quip.

"Right, Milo," Rosa said, running a hand over her exhausted face, "the place we are going is one you've never been, so it is impossible for you to picture it. But I have an idea. I think given we've seen evidence that the orbs I touched earlier charged almost instantaneously and fueled the Quip so well, I am hoping that if we link hands as I imagine our destination, and you try to keep your mind clear, I will be able to supply the picture and take us there, just as we can take someone with us when we bookwander. Try not to feel any pressure. If it doesn't work, we can walk, but I believe in you, Milo. You can do this. You're the Quip's Driver and she listens to you. You just need to point her toward what's going on in my imagination."

"Okay." Milo nodded, not saying that telling him to not feel any pressure was a little useless.

He held out his hand, and Rosa took it firmly. She gave him a small smile and a nod, and they shut their eyes. Milo tried to clear his mind of anything, to not think of anywhere he had been before, to keep his mind on the Quip. But of course, when you are asked not to think of something, it is the hardest thing in the world. Images of Pages & Co. and the Underlibrary and the house he had spent his first six years in all flickered through his brain at the same time until . . .

Suddenly it was as though a current of electricity were running through him but causing no pain. He could feel a power coming from where his hand was linked with Rosa's that was clear and pure and right. His mind was simply full of imagination, just sparkling, golden possibilities. He blew hard on the Driver's whistle, and, without thinking, he knew how to ask the Quip to follow Rosa's imagination. The train glided smoothly forward as soon as he thought it.

Milo heard the others talking, but it was the faintest itch

at his concentration, just background noise. The only time he'd felt anything like this was when he lay on top of the Quip and took in the beautiful expanse of Story and all its wonder and promise. Almost as soon as they had moved, the Quip slowed to a stop, and the imagination flowed back along his arm to Rosa. He looked at her in amazement.

"Well done, Milo." Rosa smiled. "You were perfect."

They stepped out of the Quip and found themselves at a stretch of Hadrian's Wall perched on the crest of a rolling hill. A section of the wall extended out from the main stretch into a square shape, and there was what was left of an old archway. Stones curved up from a wooden gate, stones that would once have met in the middle, but now the arch was incomplete and left a gap of blue sky in between. When Milo first looked at the arch, he thought he saw the shimmer of something beyond the stones, but when he looked properly it had gone and he could just see the fields rolling out behind them.

"Here we are," Rosa said. She turned to look at the four children, and Milo couldn't work out the emotions skittering across her face. "To get through this archway, we need the Anonymous Reader," she said. "But I think that will be okay."

Milo, Alessia, and Oskar all looked at Tilly.

"What do I do?" she asked, stepping forward.

"Come, let me show you all," Rosa said, and they walked right up to the archway and its crumbling stones. She gestured at a symbol carved into one of the stones, something unfamiliar to Milo that looked ancient and mythical. "If you put your hand on there, Tilly, and think of stories and book-wandering and all they mean to you, then hopefully . . . Well, just have a go."

Milo watched as Tilly did as she was asked, placing her hand carefully over the symbol and closing her eyes tightly. But there was nothing, no shimmer or spark of book magic.

His chest tightening in worry, Milo glanced at Rosa, who to his surprise was looking straight at him. She cocked her head and smiled, to Milo's absolute confusion.

"I did wonder," Rosa said. She put a gentle hand on Tilly's shoulder and whispered something in her ear. Tilly looked surprised for just a moment but then smiled and looked at Milo as well, taking her hand from the stones.

"Ohhhh," breathed Alessia. "Of course!"

"Did—did I miss something?" Milo said. "I'm sorry, I . . ."

"I don't think you need to apologize," Oskar replied quietly, nudging him forward. It abruptly dawned on Milo why everyone was looking at him.

"Oh no," he said, stepping backward into Oskar. "No, no, no, you're wrong. It can't be me—there is literally nothing special about me."

"Milo, there is more that is special about you than you could ever possibly understand," Rosa said, kneeling down in front of him.

"But I can't do anything extra magical," he insisted. "And

look at my family, I don't come from a line of powerful booksellers or guardians of books; I come from a family of people who steal and lie and betray their friends!"

"The Anonymous Reader is not about special powers, or who your family is," Rosa said. "It has always been purely about who *you* are as a reader, and the place that stories hold in your heart. It is about caring for others and respecting that everyone has their own journey. As soon as I met you, I knew you carried the wonder of stories deep in your bones, Milo Bolt, and I have only seen and heard more since to convince me that it was you all along: the way you could lift the sword to slay the Jabberwock, the way you could feel other people's reading memories so potently, the way the Quip listens to you. It's you, Milo. I am sure of it."

He was still in a daze as Rosa shepherded him toward the stones.

"Will you try?" she asked. "It's okay if it doesn't work—it doesn't make you any less or *more* special. We will need all of our skills put together to find the Book and save bookwandering, whether your ability is this or something else."

Milo braced himself for failure, but put his hand against the symbol carved into the stone. Closing his eyes, he searched his mind to find that place he had felt onboard the Quip when he was holding Rosa's hand. And unlike last time, when Rosa had helped nudge him there, this time, he found it by himself. His mind slid into that place of clarity and power, and he could feel the magic of imagination sparking all around him, all the stories and ideas that powered life charging the air. The magic flowed from him, and he opened his eyes to see golden rivers of imagination radiating out from him into the stone arch, which was lit up from within. The symbol itself started to glow, as though filled with molten gold, and then, just as he felt the power starting to ebb, there was a flicker and a noise like the breeze through the leaves of the great sycamore tree, and the air beyond the arch started to shimmer.

The gate melted away, and the stones creaked and echoed as they built themselves up to form an unbroken arch over Milo's head. He turned round, and Tilly, Alessia, and Oskar were watching, mouths open in wonder. Rosa, however, was still looking straight at him, and gave him a smile of pride and approval he had never had from an adult before.

The shimmering looked like a veil between the stones, like the air on a hot day, and then all of a sudden the haze cleared and the fields behind the wall dissolved, to be replaced by something completely different. Even the arch itself seemed to have taken on a new aspect. The great stones now looked to be made of slate and gray rock, and through the arch weren't grass and sheep but the sea. A path of golden sandy stone stretched in front of them, bending away from view, and then beyond, just a few feet away, was the ocean. They could hear seagulls keening, smell the seaweed on the air and taste the salt on their lips.

"It worked," Rosa breathed in relief.

"Where is that?" Milo asked, feeling a little faint from opening the gateway.

"Through there is King Arthur's castle," Rosa said. "Where myths were born and bookwandering was breathed to life. Where we'll find Merlin, and *The Book of Books* that he guards. Are you ready? I cannot promise what we will discover here or how dangerous it will get."

Milo glanced at the others, who looked solemn and determined.

"For my family," said Tilly.

"For Pages & Co.," Oskar said.

"For *The Book of Books*," Alessia added.

"And for bookwandering," Milo finished.

And with that the five of them joined hands and stepped through the arch and straight into legend.

THE END

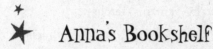 Anna's Bookshelf

The bookwandering we see the characters in the Pages & Co. series do is into old books. This is because there are rules about using other people's stories and ideas, and you're only allowed to do it seventy years after an author has died (ninety-five years in the US). I love the books that I have my characters bookwander into, but here are some books that are more recent that I've loved reading and think you might too:

Charmed Life by Diana Wynne Jones
The Skylarks' War by Hilary McKay
The Good Turn by Sharna Jackson
Frankie Best Hates Quests by Chris Smith
The Phantom Tollbooth by Norton Juster
Front Desk by Kelly Yang
The Storm Keeper's Island by Catherine Doyle
Rooftoppers by Katherine Rundell

Amari and the Night Brothers by B. B. Alston

Rumaysa by Radiya Hafiza

Me, My Dad and the End of the Rainbow
   by Benjamin Dean

The Hatmakers by Tamzin Merchant

The Midnight Guardians by Ross Montgomery

The Island at the End of Everything
   by Kiran Millwood Hargrave

The Legend of Podkin One-Ear by Kieran Larwood

Acknowledgments

Thank you to Claire Wilson, my agent, for your constant support, wisdom, and kindness, and thank you to everyone at RCW, in particular Safae El-Ouahabi and David Dunn.

Thank you to everyone at my publisher, HarperCollins Children's Books. Firstly, thank you to some people who have been integral to Pages & Co. and who have now moved on from HCCB: Julia Sanderson, I will miss you very much; thank you for everything you've done and for being such a pleasure to work with. Louisa Sheridan, beloved publicist and person—I do not know what I am going to do without you. Samantha Stewart, for being so wise and kind, whether things were going smoothly or otherwise. And Ann-Janine Murtagh, thank you for having faith in my books from the outset.

Thank you to my editor, Nick Lake, who understands how stories work so beautifully; I am very grateful that I have you to help me work out how to tell mine. Thank you, Rachel Quin, Laura Hutchison, Alex Cowan, Jess Dean, Elisa Offord, Elorine Grant, Megan Reid, Francesca Lecchini-Lee, Carla Alonzi, Elizabeth Vaziri Fabio Bettin, Rob Smith, Anneka Sandher and Samantha Lacey, and everyone at HCCB.

Thank you always to Lizzie Clifford, Sarah Hughes, and Rachel Denwood.

Thank you to all my foreign publishers, in particular thank you to Cheryl Eissing, Tessa Mesicheid, and the team at Philomel Books.

Thank you to Marco Guadalupi for your beautiful illustrations and being so wonderful to work with; I'm so appreciative of the care you put into bringing Pages & Co. to life. Thank you to Paola Escobar for your work on the first three books.

Thank you to every teacher, bookseller, and librarian who has recommended and championed Pages & Co., and helped it find its way to young readers—I am so grateful.

Thank you to my friends and family; to my mum and dad and sister Hester, and the Cottons/Colliers/Bishops/Rices. Thank you always to Adam, for the love and joy you bring to our life, and the belief you have in me.

Finally, thank you to every bookwanderer, young and old, who believes in the magic of stories.

THE PAGE&

...ND CO. SERIES